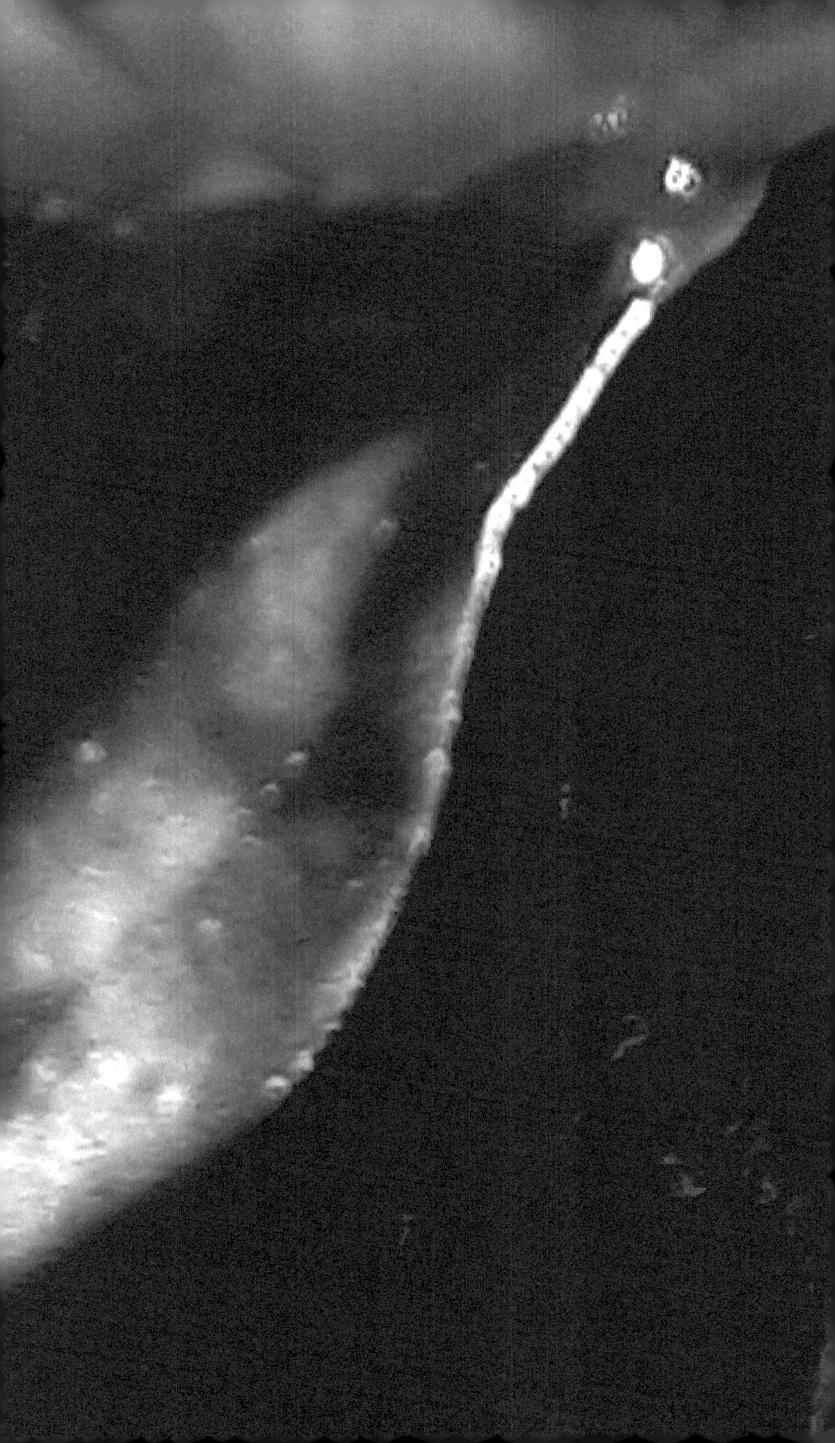

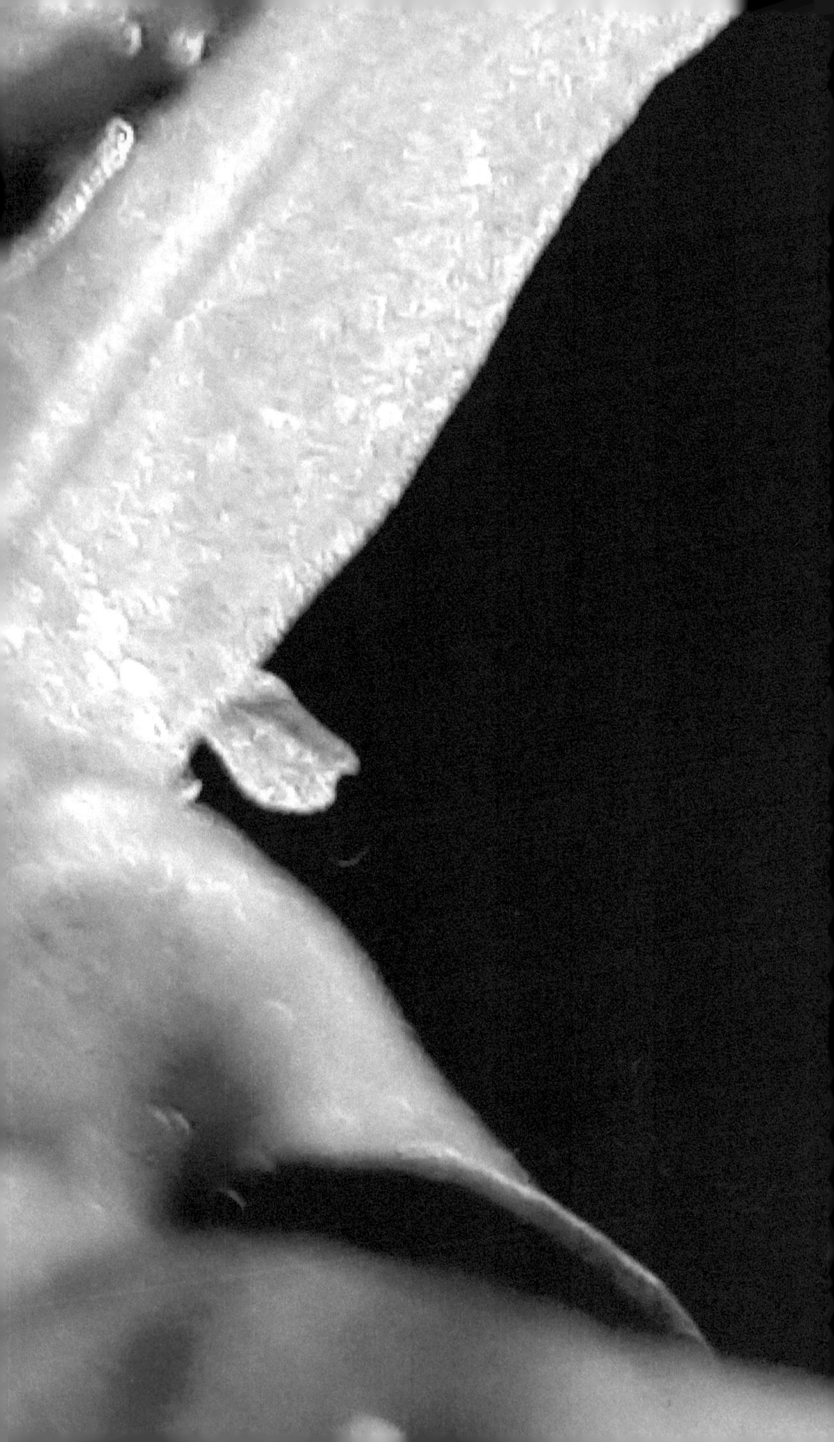

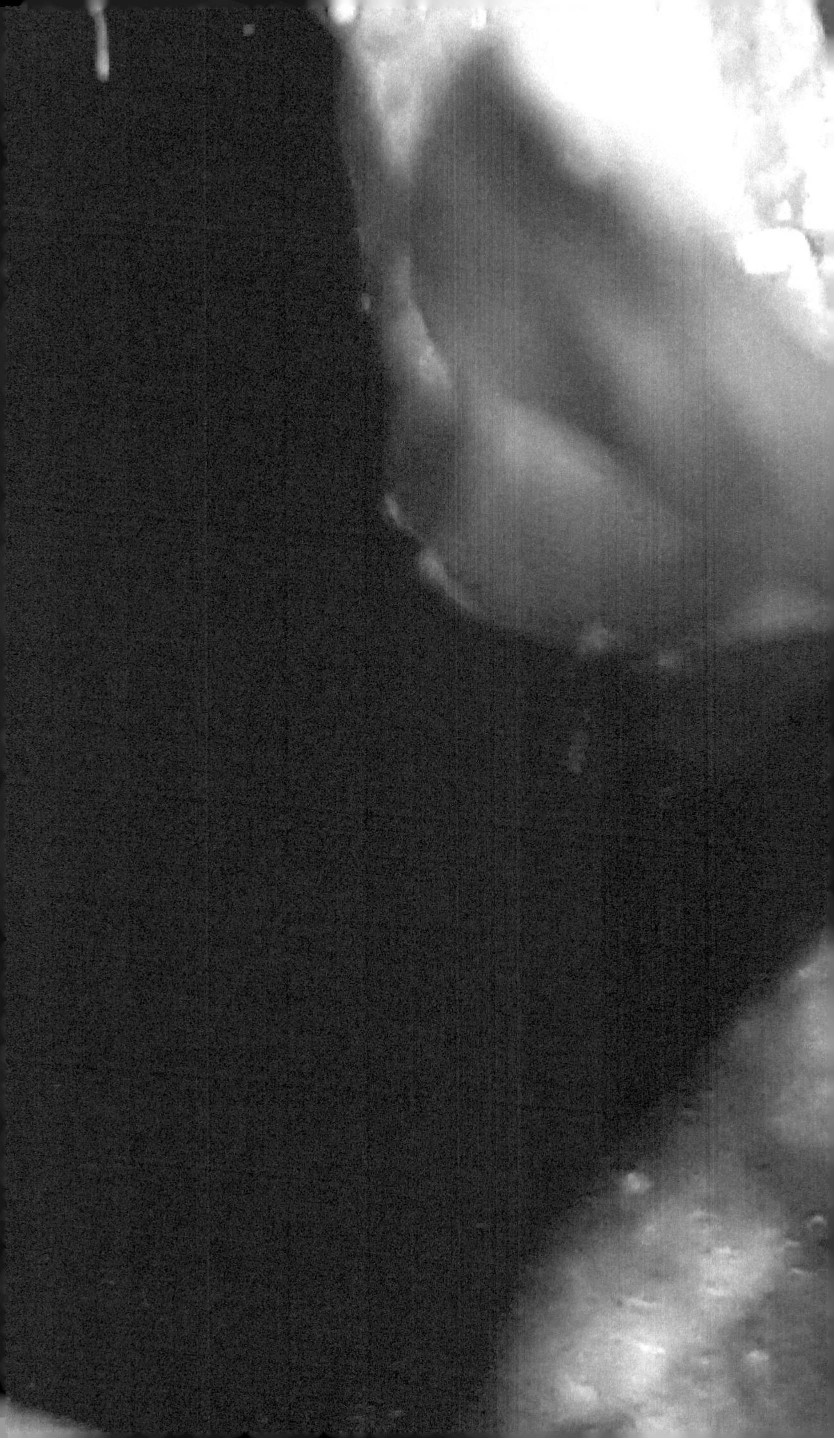

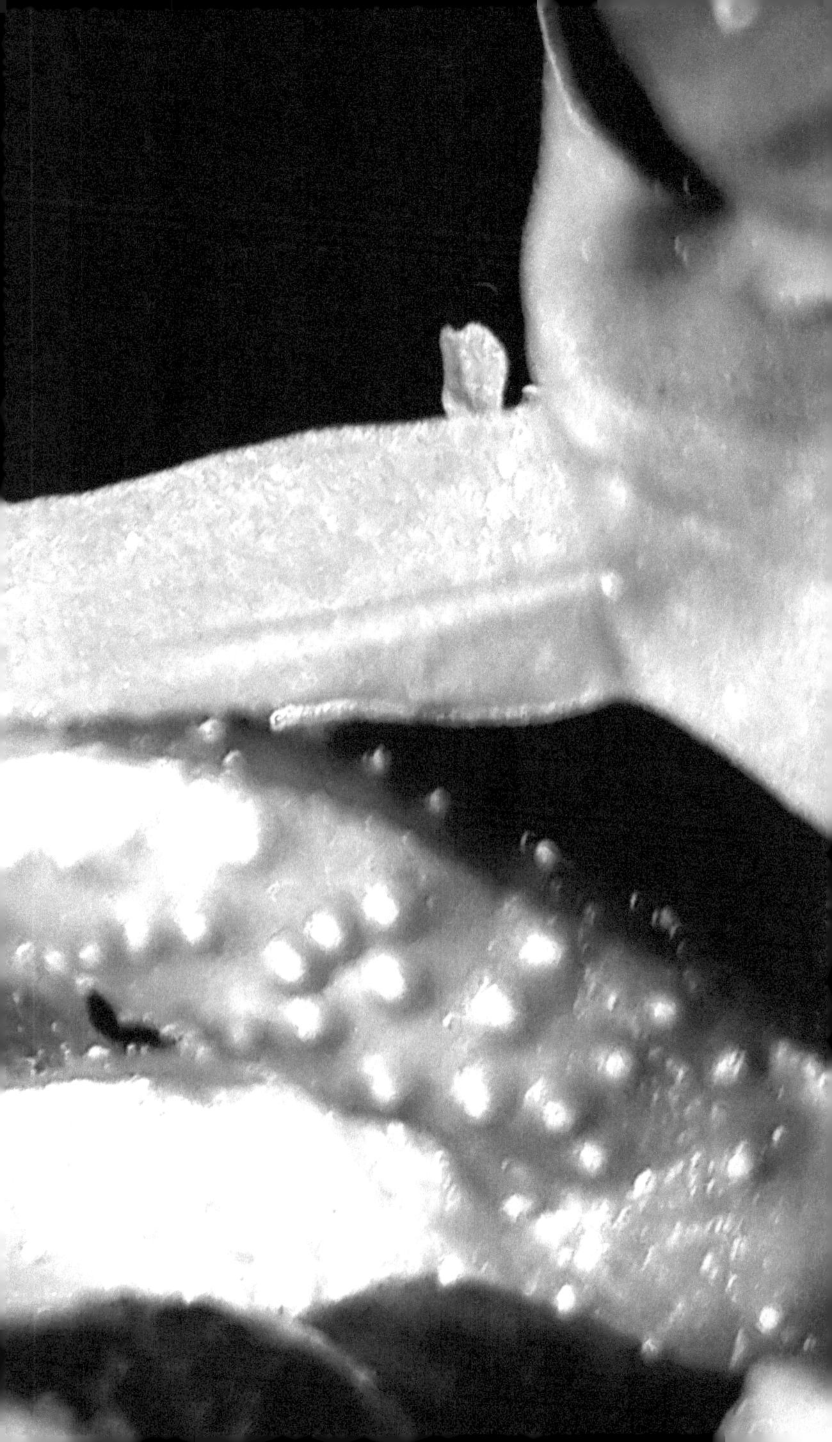

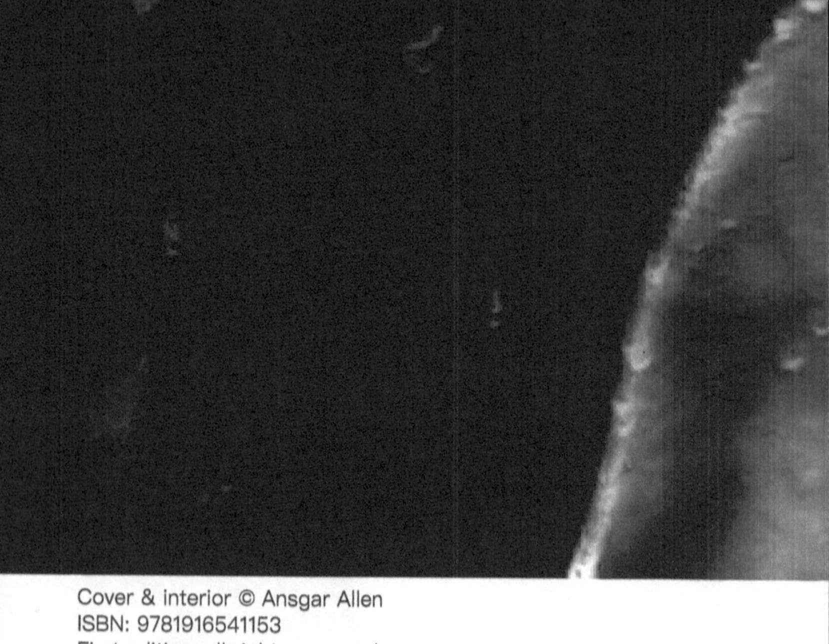

MIDDEN HILL

Ansgar Allen

Where there is dirt there is a system.
Mary Douglas

FIRST CONTACT WITH THE PATIENT.

By the time I arrived the patient was in a weak condition, his situation worsened by the purges and vomits. Their primitive understanding of the human body had them administer the very treatments they were advised to take previously, when ill, though their illnesses surely bore no relation to his and so their remedies would do nothing but damage him further. We purged and vomited him one said, telling me with obvious pride as the other three stood by in agreement. I listened to them tell me about their purging and the manner of their purging, and their vomiting and the techniques they employed, and wondered just what they had themselves been purged and vomited for. It had clearly done them no good.

His clothes were removed and his body disentangled from the weed—this much they achieved. But even that doing of theirs was negligible. It was doubtful they had done it at all. I was told they removed his clothes as they were sodden and the man was suffering from the cold. They told me he was better off naked. It was not only for the purging and vomiting they took them off, they said. These clothes were removed even before they lifted him, it was the first thing they did. We did it after we unwound the weed. It was done where the tide had left him. Only when drawn back to his nakedness did they raise him up.

We saw his condition was bad and so we took extra care. Once we glimpsed his skin we decided against reclothing, they said as I listened without comment. They would not give him any of their own because they feared for the cloth. It was out of the question to donate any of ours. They did have spares, we keep them in that trunk they told me indicating the trunk. We each have a second set they said then opening the trunk to show them off. These were folded, or bunched all four, a second outfit for each lined up from one end of the trunk to the other. It would have been possible, we could have easily done it, we have the clothes we could give him and would have given them willingly, only, our clothes would stick just as his old clothes did stick, and so he was better off without. He would have to dry naturally, they decided. The skin must be allowed to dry we said.

We stood up and told those who gathered round, Move back give the man some space. Move out so the wind can get him. Let the sun reach him. The sun must touch his skin. Only after the rawness is gone can he be covered we told them. We knew his skin must be deprived of its moistness, that his skin must give its water to the air and that it might even begin to crack before we could allow any material to touch down upon it. Not even our hands should do so. Our hands cannot touch him without doing harm we said to those assembled. Our hands, we said holding them up, cannot touch him. Perhaps only our fingertips might do we then ventured. It might be that only our fingertips will touch him. It would only worsen his condition, they added, looking at me, the physician. As soon as his clothes were gone it would be possible for the wind and sun to do their work. And so it was, the wind and sun did begin to dry his skin. But that was not all. His rawness ensured the skin became wet again with its own juices they said looking at me, but then the sun dried that up too and gradually dried up the juices of his skin. This was how the wetness returned by the drawing of juices to replenish its loss. His clothes entrapped him, gathered his secretions, and so halted them, and thereby prevented the actions of the elements. We would allow the elements to act, we decided. Move back and allow the elements in we might have said although we did not say it and only thought of saying it. We each only thought it, one said as the other three nodded. We each of us knew about the elements, the next told me. We knew that the elements were needed. As we removed those clothes with our fingertips, we came to realise the necessity of it, they told me, and saw the importance of not leaving a scrap.

They used different words, rudimentary words, rural hamlet words. But in its core, this is what they expressed with irrepressible circularity. They used their best words and delivered those words to me with their best elocution, yet still these and the expressions they resorted to were rough and limited. Their words were plain but recursive. Their words gathered and were soon stacked together, exhibiting a recursive tendency and a stacking tendency which betrayed the essential stasis of their rural hamlet life.

We began to unclothe him, they went on in their rural hamlet way. We began to unclothe him and then realised we must unclothe him. As we continued we realised there was no stopping until he was entirely undone and there was not a piece of material left over. This was the first decisive thing we did for his recovery. When we unclothed him we saved him they declared as I sat listening and as I continued to decipher their repetitive, recursive, rural hamlet speech, a language confined and developed in isolation at the edges of our land, a solidified speech of a coastline outlook that remained evasive so long as it was not transposed, a language that is basically deceptive, which contains hidden inlets—as our own language might say— and could only be properly rendered and sufficiently understood by translating it into my own. I listened to their rural hamlet words saying nothing to encourage them further. They encouraged themselves well enough by speaking.

I asked the woman at the inn who said she watched it all. She told me his clothes largely removed themselves. The four of them did not unclothe him, she said, telling me this by her own version of their rural hamlet speech. There was no way they unclothed him, she told me after I relayed their account to her so I might judge her, and judge them, from her reaction. She joined the crowd of onlookers and watched as they leant over the man who had washed up on the beach. She watched as they took possession of the man as theirs to save. When she saw them leaning over the body, taking possession, she noticed his clothes were effectively peeling off on their own. So too perhaps the weed cracked and flaked away, but about that she said nothing. Leaning as they did over the body, the four had little much to do except take possession of it. All they did was take the body up. Any other claim is embellishment, she said, or used a word meaning something like it, an equivalent more closely matched to the rudiments of her environment. We have so few visitors. Hardly ever anyone of outside here from sea or overland. When they saw the body they decided it was theirs and the rest of us would not have a hold, a touch, or a poke about it. We came down soon enough but only got pieces. As soon as we noticed the body by the water we were on our way across the beach. But the four arrived first and so the body was theirs. They say they unclothed him but all they did was pick material off him. They picked at it, she said, and raised the fragments to the little crowd about them.

They presented these fragments as curiosities, she told me, so the crowd might marvel at their rottenness, their substitute for touching. The four merely peeled the last from his body and as they did took off some parts of the underlying skin. There was no unclothing of the man. They did not unclothe him, she confirmed, nor did they reveal anything any of us did not already know from seeing. The condition of his skin was revealed before them, the basic surface of the man and his extruding wetness was never hidden and was obvious to us all. We stood close by. We came close as we were able, close as they allowed with their arms stretched backward. We were close enough to see the condition of it even before the weed was taken off and the last fragments of fabric were peeled away. We all knew as we stood right about, she said. The four did not reveal it to us and they did not save him from it.

When I asked her just what these remaining fragments indicated, she was silent. I mean the fragments of fabric you held as they were passed around. What did they indicate regarding his occupation, I added. What did they state regarding his social position or his place of origin. Was he foreign. Did the clothing indicate he was from a different land or was he of our own. Was he a foreigner, I repeated. Did he seem to you a foreigner, I said to her. Did you get any sense that he was from someplace else very different. Was he dressed like us or was he dressed like another people. To which all there was no adequate reply. I received no proper response as the landlady stood, impossibly close, holding an egg in one hand, peeling it with the other. I asked about the fabric and its origins and she went on peeling to the white. All she said regarding and in response to my line of questioning was that they stated nothing about any of it. When I pushed the point about describing me any clue how he was once shod, seeking any detail at all however minor from the fragments that were passed about, the landlady replied whilst holding the egg how the seawater had corrupted the fabric of his vestments to such an extent it was no longer possible to determine his occupation or standing or origin or religion or culture or any of that you would have me know from what remained. Or this effectively is what I gathered. Even the colour of the fragments was indeterminate, she said. They were the colour of rot, she told me, which to a physician means almost any of the browns, greens, yellows, and necrotic blues.

When given the opportunity to tell a bit more of what they had done the four replied they could not remember the nature of the clothes they removed, even though they remembered quite precisely how they removed them. They told me at length once again of the unclothing, how they did not slightly shift him as they did so, not even roll him this way or that to take it all off, but managed to say absolutely nothing about the concealments they released him of. This corroborated the landlady's story. There could be nothing to remember if the clothes were not fit for removal, if there was no removing them because the clothes were rotten and fallen off. The man was never disrobed, I knew.

He was carried by the four of us to the house, they said. To the awe of the crowd they took him with them. We took him with us and the crowd looked on. They stood up decisively and carried him off the beach. We stood up decisively, they said. The crowd was most of all struck by how we raised him after we ourselves stood up and then bent down and lifted him to shoulder height. They saw how we raised him up without hardly shifting him from his position as he had lain on the beach. As we did so, as we stood and then lifted him to our shoulders, they were taken along by how delicately we managed it. He did not shift at all. We held him at shoulder height exactly as he had lain on the beach. It was impossible but we managed it. We ventured to raise him up without a single limb shifting from its place. Not one arm dropped or thigh fell. It was improbable but we did it and we did so to the awe of all who watched. They trailed us from the beach and then gathered from the passages and alleys of the small fishing hamlet as we passed through not one arm shifting or leg sliding. He lay still as he did when we found him. The crowd only grew as we left the sands.

The four brought him up here, so they said, to this place where I first met my patient, and they laid him in a cot and covered him with sackcloth. When we purged and vomited him outside his limbs did now shift. It was unavoidable that his aspect changed when we did that. And as we carried him up the stairs his body changed its aspect again. We turned him over and moved his body and his limbs through the narrow space just there where you see us pointing and around the landing. How he lies here in his cot is not how he lay on the beach. But until that point, and from the beach to the threshold of our house for sure, he was unmoved and remained as the sea had last decided. We merely raised him up to the awe of all onlookers. When we delivered him to this room, and when we put the cloth over, he was at last dried sufficiently, they said, looking at me the physician, expecting my approval once more. His skin was dry enough for the sackcloth they told me indicating the sackcloth. When I failed to look over at the cloth, the four gestured again. Look how it did not congeal to his skin, they said, lifting it slightly. We judged it perfectly. We only laid a cover once he was in the house and the crowd was gone. After the crowd was gone, we covered him up.

THE LIMBS THE WAIST THE CHEST AND THE NECK.

I looked at the cover, the sackcloth they laid down on him. It was an insult to any man, I thought. These lives were basic but there was linen in the house. As I lifted the cover and glimpsed his body I was myself struck by the condition of his skin, blistered, resembling bladder wrack or black tang in hue and deformity. Although it was kelp, so they thought, which entangled him and thereby saved him at sea, keeping afloat and carrying over the waves and finally drawing him across the rocks and sand and shingle. He came ashore in broad sweeps and retreats attached by the weed not wrack to the wreck of a coble. There was so much of it, he must have passed through a vast quantity of weed to become entangled like that. Forests of weed like this would be needed to tie him so well and forests like that do not exist here in our waters but they do exist out at sea and can surround islands, they went on. He was bound to its remaining timbers by the limbs and the waist and the chest and the neck. He was held this way and that is what kept him from swallowing the waters. Because of the weed he was saved. When we found him, we disentangled him. These ligatures once permitted his survival yet now served to garrotte or hold him into stillness against his greater weight. On land the weed endangered him, it threatened to strangle him, whereas at sea the very same entanglement saved him, restricting his breathing most probably, and yet through that restriction and by holding his head it kept him alive. What might kill on land surely saved at sea. We freed him of it and that is how he lived. This was how they found him I was told again and as they went on. Before unclothing him they had to release him from the wreck of the coble against which he was tied. As he lay on the beach he lay attached to that wreck by the limbs and the waist, the chest and the neck. This was the position they then raised him in, his head still held back and bent to the side, his limbs twisted as they had been positioned when they were bound. When they hoisted him to their shoulders he was still in the bound line that his body had suffered, forced alongside the planks by each ligature that pulled the neck outward and round and the palms outward too and the belly outward also as each followed the contours of the wreckage.

The cot he lay in might seem a mercy after the peeling the drying the carrying and the purging and the vomiting they performed before bringing him in.

The latter was just before the house. They purged and vomited by its small entrance and as the crowd looked on. None of the purges or the vomits were there when I arrived. They said they cleared them away and took them to the dumping ground by the river, effectively a kind of midden where all the refuse and slop of the hamlet, mainly fish carcases, the occasional dog, and other wastes were thrown. I should have gone to inspect these purges and vomits but the lot would be covered over.

We placed him here so he might have some rest before you arrived, they said, looking at me the physician for approval. But the cot itself endangered him, I knew, as lying flat will endanger any patient ill enough to require it. Confinement to bed is a pernicious choice even if putting to bed is the only option available for the severely ill. Taking to bed may be the single only choice but will always be a deadly one given how the laying of a patient thickens the juices and enfeebles the solid parts. These become indolent at their edges and begin to disintegrate. The erect posture that the upright hominids have adopted—a conceit shared with the penguin, writes Magellan—has become necessary to their health, which is why the sick, when laid flat and often with no other recourse for sure, are tended to become more sick. Pillows may be stuffed to raise a little, yet the sick will be made sicker, and this despite the expert ministrations and remedies of the doctor. And it will happen because of the simple fact of their first lying down. My work as a medical practitioner reaches its natural limit in the event of laying flat. My work reaches its limit even when the patient is moderately inclined. Most patients are already laid out before I arrive and no longer have the strength to stand and will not even be commanded to sit. When I arrive, I should say to those assembled, But you laid the patient and this limits what I can do. Inevitably I say nothing of the sort although I begin my work thinking that, knowing that. Because the patient is confined to bed the patient will become bedridden. The solid parts will already be weakened and will have begun dissolving and the juices thereabout quantifiably thickened. If I do not tell the family or whoever has laid the patient down that what they did worsened the situation, I do indeed tell myself, This limits what I can do. I arrive, see the patient, look at those assembled and think, This limits me for sure.

Determining that his condition was untreatable and death was assured, I should have left. It was obvious as I entered the room that I should leave right soon after because there was nothing I could do. As usual they had laid their invalid flat and left him in that position as if being still, and being horizontal, were the route to recovery rather than its opposite. But I sent the carriage away. This was to the relief of the whip who was intent on returning before nightfall. He did not fancy the prospect, so he told me. I have no intention of returning after dark, the whip said repeatedly on the journey over. He was quite resolved about that.

As I sat in the rear of the coach clutching my doctor's bag he turned and addressed me as his doctor. My doctor, he said from up front, we must not return after dark. Look doctor, the whip went on, not after dark is all there is to be said on the matter, because look at that, he remarked each time we passed some obstacle that might break the wheels or some rut that might turn us over or precipice down which we might fall. Look at that, he declared, and tell me you would have us return after dark. See that rut and tell me you would have us travel back without seeing it approach. See that precipice and honestly confess to me now with it here before you and not behind you in your memory that it would not bother you at all to be travelling here, on this very track, at this very point, after dark. I would rather not and surely you must agree. Even with the moon there is no avoiding that rock, that rut, that precipice. We must not return after nightfall. It would be fatal to. And so on we went with him turned about, looking at me, telling it so. My very own doctor, he went on, we must depart before nightfall, long before dark in fact, he added. We must leave so there is enough daylight left to make it across the moors when the sun is up, or across the worst sections, if only the present sections. We must get along these present ones right here, the sections of the track we are currently picking our way across. These are surely the worst sections, the most dangerous if not the most obviously fatal sections of our journey. These are absolutely fatal, he assured me. If we do not take sufficient care they will teach us their lesson. There is a fatal lesson at every bend. This entire route is a fatal lesson. These sections, he said, turning back at me once more, these sections are absolutely so. I have seen fatal accidents all along this stretch. Each precipice has seen one, I suspect, said he, and many of them I have witnessed. Over there is a fatal accident and there is another one he told me as we turned the next bend. That, my doctor, was a fatal accident, and so is this. He indicated every possible danger as we travelled on, referring to each fatal accident which we passed as we went on our way, every fatal turn that would finish us off, that would surely finish us off, he said. This one would do us in for certain, he told me, pointing out a rock, a rut, a precipice. It would surely kill us if I cannot see our passage and steer us clear. These moors, he said, and this track especially are fatal. Listen doctor, he told me, it is important you understand me plainly now. Listen to me and hear what I have to say. Even during the day they are fatal and will finish you off for a moment's inattention, the whip said, turning his head right back so that he could address me, rotating the body by shifting his legs on the box seat so he could fully address me and press the importance of what he had to tell. Even during the day, he said. During the day every stretch and turn and rut that I have described to you is a fatal accident if I do not look out. He sat on his box seat, his body twisted, his legs shifted towards me, and turned himself entirely round at the shoulders to tell me that, to face me and tell me this as the coach was propelled on by his horse and not by the reins, these, themselves, inattentively rested across his hands. We made much of our way by the good sense and habits of the beast, by its enduring wit to haul at the width of our four wheels and nothing less, because anything less than what they spanned could be fatal as the coachman had said. We relied for good stretches of that passage, so I thought, on its good reckoning or at least its lucky reckoning of the width of the cart and the whims of the vehicle that had its own motions too. These demanded accounting for as it rocked and pivoted on its springs and axles and as the wheels pivoted and wobbled in turn. We owed to the beast more than the whip. And so when it came to my own decisive moment I was glad to send the coachman away and accept the generosity of my hosts, such as it was. They made ready for my stay in the extent of their resources as I sat with the patient to examine further.

This region of coast has presented me before with abject specimens, patients who came ashore suffering from the sea air and its noxious effects, which, when taken in too deeply, can cause a disequilibrium in the economies of its hosts. Looking at this particular example of human suffering, I could see it presented a difficult case and was of a type I had not yet seen. Noxious air will affect the blood and the animal juices and obstruct the whole system, the nerves particularly. Its consequences are by no means easy to combat. But the man before me suffered differently still. His internal economy was disturbed neither by dampness nor by wind or by rolling about at sea—the effects of which I know well and well know how to treat. As I have witnessed, these disturbances are received into our habit, become mixed with our fluids, and are characterised in ways I am trained to reckon. Certain minerals that seep from the base of the cliff and pervade the waters of the tides are also known to impregnate the body, as evidenced most commonly by blackened organs or some degree of putrefaction, but again I sensed nothing of that kind here. Neither the drained flesh of the freezing sea nor the fiery particles of perpetual sun had left their mark. I have seen nitrous effluvia sucked into the body and what that brings forth to the mouth. I have witnessed the effects of foul linen, such as which rotted from his body, and have seen its imprint upon skin that yields to the putrefaction of the cloth, yet it hardly compared to his condition. His hands and feet, and then his legs and arms, and the stomach and shoulders were swelled due to their contact with the water, since water will penetrate a pig's bladder and finds no obstruction when faced with the pores of the skin. But the skin of wrecked sailors and fishermen has never come to resemble contours of this type.

If anything, and excepting the most obvious lesions, he had more of the condition of the sedentary, studious type I have treated inland, the vicar's son the latest case, although the son's suffering was directly relatable to his reading, and so, with the cause made known, was quickly remedied. I visited and noted the viscous and heavy fluids that plagued him and distorted his vision. I told his father, the vicar, of the fluids and their languid movement, of the oppressive tumult of his mind and its fixations, and the black train of evil from which his son must be fenced if he was to survive the week. The vicar took my advice with due seriousness and exacted his remedy. He drew it from the words I had spoken and their implications and his son's sickness receded soon after my advice was taken. It is no exaggeration to claim his son was rescued from oblivion by my visit. Upon my departure the vicar prohibited all ungodly texts and laid them out for the cattle to trample. He had his boy labour and live with the poorest folk, those who will heave and drag for a living. He had him live like that, heaving and dragging, until his son was cured. It was rumoured the folk his son worked with did subsequently display traces of the visit long after the son left and was re-united with his father, and that the sickness was among them.

There was also the case of the young teacher who came to live with his grandparents. I visited the old folks in the house below, with the grandson remaining in their attic. The recluse had not descended the attic ladder for several weeks accepting occasionally the merest morsel as evidenced too by the man no longer hardly needing his toilet. He first went above telling the old couple below that he was decided on writing a book. This book the young teacher had in mind to write would rival in its imaginative fancy all the stranger works of antiquity and naturally the more ordinary ones too would be each robustly superseded by the young man's efforts. Once his own was finally written, if any book could be found surpassing his feat that greater book could only be the work of the gods, the young teacher told them much to their disdain. His grandfather stood by the hatch and told the man that he too had once been taken with the idea of producing something new, but that his grandson should reckon with two things. First, the gods if they were indeed gods would have nothing to do with men. And second, the imagination will ever only achieve little without them. His grandfather told the recluse above that when he had once written, back when he was still driven to write, he had himself witnessed in his own productions how little his imagination could do. I saw what little my imagination could do, the old man said, and was sure to always do a little less. I came to the limits of my imagination, the old man called up with an old man's hoarseness, and knew the only thing that could be done in the face of those limits is to aim a little lower. We must always aim a little lower, he shouted up, pleading with his grandson to come back down and join him and his grandmother who was very sick now indeed with the anguish of it all, reminded at each moment lest she ever become distracted by the sound of their grandson stalking above. I was not taken in, the old man said, and neither should you be deceived by the fond delusion that the writer can travel wherever they please and create whatever they wish. The writer travels nowhere and accomplishes nothing that is not already there, in some form, and this nothing hardly warrants saying. It has always been the devil's trickery to think that something can be written from that nothing much we are. When I wrote, the old man said, back when I was still given to writing, I always travelled short of what I had the potential for and created a little less. I thought it better to exercise restraint and reign myself in prematurely. Always aim a little lower. See what little you can achieve and do a bit less. Naturally the old man's council achieved nothing itself and the grandson remained above rocking about in the eves and upon the rafters, driving himself into a frenzy no doctor would have within his power to abate. My advice to the old folk was very simple. It was to weaken the ceiling above the young teacher's bedchamber, and do so quietly, and by degrees and by nibbling the wood of the exposed beams, until at last their grandson would stride across the attic floor above that room and fall through and directly into bed. The shock of it would return the man to his senses so I said.

These were instructive cases, and yet, with my latest patient nothing could be drawn from my experiences with the vicar and his son or the young teacher and his oldfolks. It did me no good to reflect upon them. In the present case there were no readings to prohibit or stalking to abate, and so there could be no comparable remedy. I did show him God's own book, since it was laid beside him by his four hosts, but there was neither recognition expressed nor could I detect his eye gaze tracking across the pages. He did not shrink from it either.

I sat with him that first night and pondered on the evils that penetrated his cavities just as much as they plagued his surfaces. The high tide could be discerned in its movements as it rose to the edges of the village, eventually reaching up the launch by the jetty, licking froth at its furthest climb, until the sound of the waters receded and the tide fell out, elevating rocks by a creeping retreat and draining the pools to their apportionment. Seen again on my descent to the hamlet that day, those high cliffs, closed in on both sides, their bases buffered and bloated by fallen rock. The moors crept down the hills that lifted behind. Small trees leant over their edges, defunct roots reaching outward across the seaward precipice, the clods of earth they once held to fallen and gone. When the sea receded beyond earshot that night the sound of the cliffs replaced its scored rhythms. These were intermittent, short interruptions to the night as overhangs collapsed and faces sheared off and descended to rocks and scree. A perpetual fall, yet the cliffs remained only a little retreated.

I bandaged his extremities to keep them in a state of compression that would prevent any further eruption. His right fist would not open and so I bandaged it shut to heal so much as it could, undisturbed in that clenched position. His eyes remained open and wandering until finally, by morning, they were fixed on me as I woke in my chair. These eyes then rose with me as I stood to examine. His mouth moved and I leant over to listen to him speak the first sounds of which I shall presently describe. His skin had recovered so well that by the third day I could remove the bandages and marvel at my good sense in applying a remedy, that of compression, which took effect more quickly than any doctor might ever hope when confronted by what I had seen. One hand remained open, the other stiff. His condition was still poor, his suffering unusual, unlike so many I have tended who decline and worsen in ways that are completely ordinary and which I have seen so often. In light of my experiences of so much ordinary suffering the great novelty of his illness was worth recording, so I felt, and this helped reconcile me to staying beyond the point where death seemed assured and so was not worth attending. My doctor friends and I have a phrase we share just between us for this condition, our bit of wit—The living remains of the departed, we call it—which is also, and somewhat inevitably, the signal of our own departure. We report to one another the cases we have seen and we tell of this or that case of Living Remains and how we departed upon seeing these Remains of the Departed and how there was no option but departure given the state of the Living Remains we were confronted with as we opened the door, as we were presented with the patient, and as we use that phrase between ourselves we laugh a bit to lighten the mood, perhaps, enjoying once more our macabre bit of wit which binds us together in our profession. In his case however, and with the coachman gone, the point was reached against my own expectations where the phrase outlived its truth. The threat of death departed and the patient made a completely unexpected and comparatively strong outward recovery even if he remained profoundly bedridden and so was endangered by that simple fact alone. I decided it was necessary both as a medical practitioner and as a student of medical science to record his illness in the stages of its departure. It is well known that the departure of a sickness may well trace in reverse order the sequence of events by which it arrived, and thus the course of recovery can give a fair account of what occurred during the process of falling sick. I kept a close record of his suffering and its reversals for this reason, seeking to penetrate the events of his sickening. Nonetheless, his verbal account came to its own alongside my medical notes. The account he gave of his experiences gained its significance at first in whisper and then with increased strength and vigour.

There is a topography of sickness. It appears in each outward trace of a patient's imprisonment by their pain and discomfort. In some cases this becomes a pain-induced hallucination, or a pain-made seeing which paints its world over and in his case became a distinct hallucinatory myth. This account is a projection of his deranged interior, I freely admit, yet a projection which must surely change and pass beyond my own intentions as it touches outward the surfaces of his feeling so extended. His body sickness and his mind sickness could be read backwards from what he told me, indeed what he told me in this respect was far greater in its detail and consequence than my own more superficial observations of his body can allow. I must acknowledge his rendering did eventually surpass my own and has come to replace it. I include only my first observations on the extent of his bodily decline, its external symptoms, its outward lesions and dismemberments, so that his own narrative of descent into the lower reaches of human existence, consciousness, and animal perception may be contextualised. This is a record of his bodily and mental imprisonment for those who study the mind just as they study the body. And for those fewer still who study the mind in order to study the body by proxy. For those, even fewer again, who will treat the former to satisfy the latter and would thereby control them both. To the benefit of my profession, I submit this account, to treat human disorder in all its forms and without recoil and approach the excesses of the mind as it does the suppurations of the body, as a superabundance of bile that requires an outlet and must be allowed its release under supervision, or by guidance requiring a kind of incision, a necessary violence only doctoring may give. Each must be served to vent itself, and the vented substances examined. All filth is symptomatic. If present patients are too ill to be saved, their ejecta may be seen for what it can tell of those who will follow.

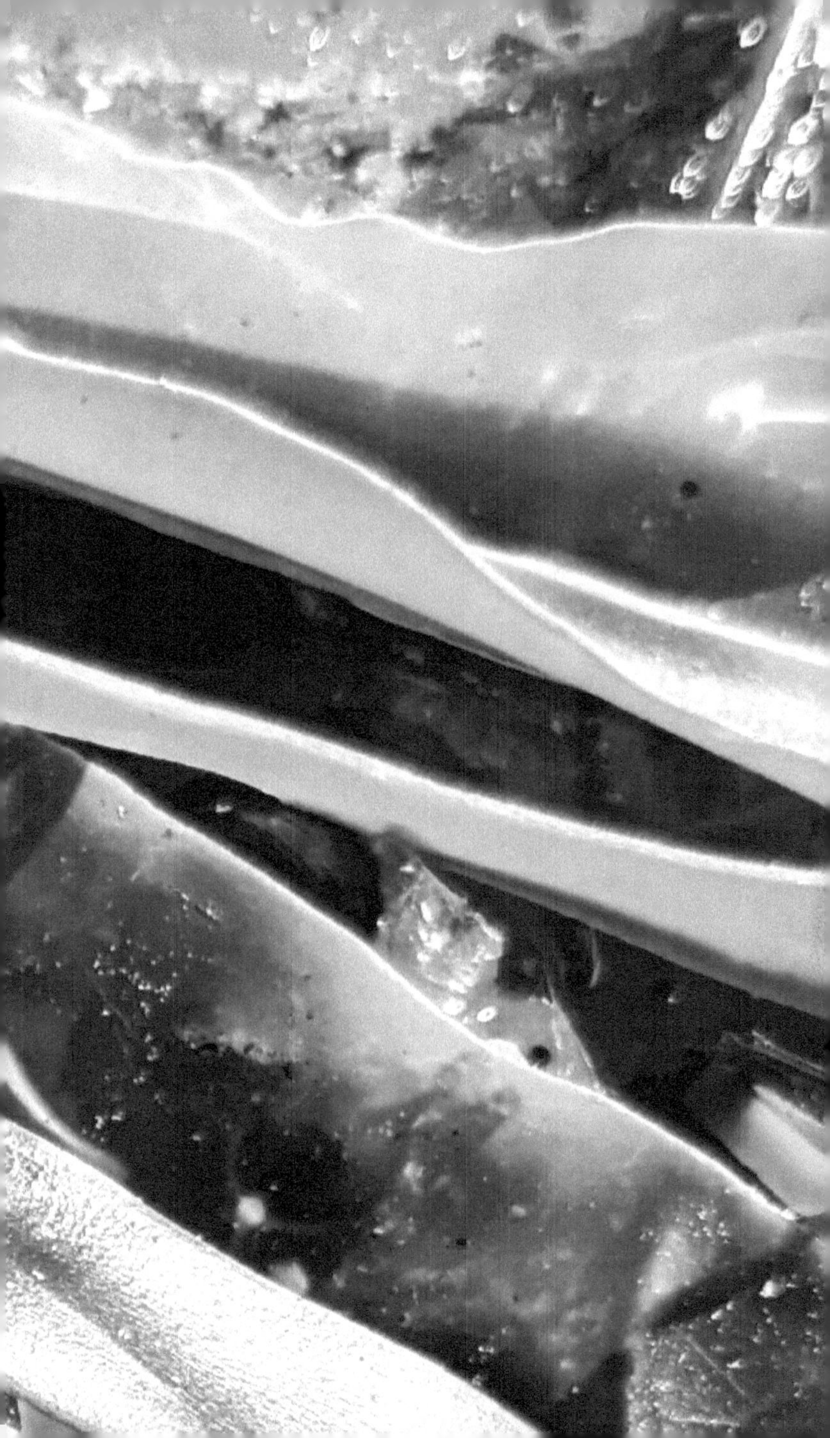

The development of speech.

His first utterances were not words but noises of the throat similar to the sound of choking. I was alarmed and opened the mouth to check his passage was clear, which it was. The tongue was in position, held forward as it should be. It took effort to overcome my curiosity and professional reflexes at the noise he made and not open the mouth to inspect again and again for choking as was my habit. He would make the sound and I would stand, ready to inspect the mouth, the throat, the airways, and then I would sit back down having remembered I had decided to no longer inspect the mouth, the throat, the airways, and only listen. He made it again and I stood again, frustrated that decision and action are not easily aligned. My decision had not yet become my action as action usurped decision. Eventually, when the sound occurred, I no longer stood and merely sat listening to it develop from a choking noise to a clicking, again from the back of the throat. If I made a similar sound the imitation I made encouraged him to repeat. I imitated his condition of not-choking whilst sounding as if he were choking, and of clicking from the back of the throat, and he made the sound of choking when not choking and clicked from the throat as if in reply. I varied my responses and he varied his. These clicks developed in complexity so that some clicks were grouped together and others were isolated, as though the silence between them signified something different. These longer silences distinguished those clicks they marked out as of a lonelier kind from the rest of the clicks which were grouped. After that, there would be grinding of the jaw as the mouth was closed, and as it remained shut, and then the mouth would open and the clicking or the choking resume, where the movement of the mouth augmented his speech. Its grinding completed the pauses. I saw his jaws begin to operate and knew we were moving on.

During the speaking of these first utterances his gaze had a wandering tendency, it would not fix on me. Whereas when he fell silent, his gaze turned and tracked me as I moved across the room. So long as he was awake and not speaking his eyes would follow me about. I walked to the left and his gaze moved to his right and tracked me as far as it could. His pupils reached the very edges of their range and the whites emerged to their fullest extent—his head could not turn—after which I would return to the cot and then stand at the foot of it and his pupils would relax to their centre. Then he would resume clicking, or making noises of the throat, and I would walk about the room without being followed, his eye gaze now again in its wandering phase. If I waited for silence to the far left of him, his eyes sought me out when the sound stopped. These eyes did not wander in that silence but searched until they found me. They would catch me at their outermost point and stay fixated on me until his speech, such as it was, resumed, and his eyes began to wander again. Not wishing to strain his eyes I ceased this experiment and remained within the region that was roughly the centre of his gaze, or at its centre if I tilted his head slightly to the right. This reduced the effort of him finding me when his speech stopped. It allowed him to reserve his energies for where they were most needed. I stood before him and leant down as he went silent. I clicked and made noises of my own that would cause him to resume and that he would then repeat and develop and elaborate on. He would at times also open his mouth, or leave it slack, and emit no sound at all for a while but appear waiting instead for the vegetative noises of the gut to resound up and through the throat. These sounds I could not imitate. I could not will them from my own gut and did not have the requisite patience to keep my jaw in its position nor keep my alimentary canal open to the best aperture for the effect until the effect was finally arrived.

Longer sounds came after, again from the back of the throat but employing the voice. These developed to vowels of a sort, and then to those sounds that employ the rest of the mouth as his tongue came into use against teeth and palate and as his lips began to resume some kind of functional movement against each other or around the shapes of the aperture they created. About the same time I transitioned too in my encouragements, and we both of us left the back of the throat as our primary operator. The choking ceased as did the clicking and the jaw grinding. His jaws were employed with the lips and the tongue to create more complex sounds, and then assemblages, then finally words. They did so as I employed my jaws in a similar way alongside his, using my lips, the tongue, to create more complex sounds, and then my own assemblages and finally words as encouragements for him to do the same.

He seemed most particularly struck by the word mid. This word was first accidentally produced from my own lips ambulating between movements. But after his fixation, the word subsequently became midden. For some length of time these words were repeated between us, alternating between mid when he was fatigued, and midden when he had the energy. I fed him words as I fed him food, mashed against the back of a spoon and mixed with those liquids he began to take down. This replaced the wetting of the lips with a damp cloth—his first sustenance. I would not attempt more than that. His first intake, the wetted cloth, was all I would risk giving him until I decided he was ready for the paste. Liquids would surely cause drowning. He had no real control of the throat and his tongue was still unreliable.

He saw me drink from a glass and I told him to take only from the cloth. This is my glass, I said, yours is the cloth. I held my glass to my lips and saw him silently watch. I lowered it and said, this water would surely drown you. Here, let me wet your lips.

It was as he came to say mid, and subsequently midden, that I gave both liquids and solids combined, worked together in the form of a paste. Then another definite word, we. He would say we and I would say we, and it subsequently became, after some variation, the more settled weed, a borrowing of mid and its mastery of the tongue tip and palate. Eventually I added the definite article, and his words became statements.

The midden, he would say and look at me through the silence these new words carried before them. The midden, he would repeat again, after which fixing his eyes on me with the look he had when first mute. The midden, he told me, as if the words themselves could communicate his meaning. The midden what, I said. The midden what, I repeated with him looking me in silence. This repeating was intended as before to encourage and extend the scope of his speech. The veins in his neck became prominent as he lifted his head—a head he could now lift. They emerged with the strings of the tendons as he struggled to inject necessary force into those words, the midden, the weed, the midden what. He spoke as if force carried meaning and his task would be accomplished by way of it. Yes, the midden, I nodded, about this midden, I said, the midden what, I repeated, and his head fell back exhausted.

As he lay his head, he regained his strength. After which he would return with the midden, or his alternative, the weed, again issued with force though not the same unsettling effect as his midden. This midden was the worse of the two. It unsettled him to say. Saying the weed was respite against saying the midden. When one disturbed him too much, he would return to the other for the break of it. The weed was hardly without significance and had its own gravity in his recollection so I felt, but against the midden it was nothing but relief. I wetted his lips between feeding him paste and waited for his returning strength as he lay his head once more.

Other words took form out of the formless silences and the raised threads of the neck, the midden what, of course, but elaborations too, as well as the occasional return of clicks and sounds of the gut, the tumult of his animal fluids and their disequilibrium. I rested in the chair and watched as he looked back, his fixed stare watching me with undiminished force. I showed him his open hand and his other, a clenched fist, and lifted his legs so he could register their recovery and draw strength from that realisation. See the hands, I said. See the legs. He could not lift them on his own. Then other words assembled, mostly disordered but a definite and growing vocabulary which subsequently came to approximate my own. These words produced longer phrases such as, dropped to the midden, or dig to the midden, or struck on the midden, phrases that not only grew in their complexity but in the satisfaction they gave him to utter.

He said such things then as dig to the midden, down on the midden, dropped to the midden, and so on, and appeared relieved he could tell it to the extent that he did and his words could manufacture. I considered his speech still infantile at this point, and listened as an adult does to a kind of babble, which is to say, not seriously enough as he himself already warranted.

Strength and some measure of dexterity returned to his unclenched hand and he gestured to himself with it, or did something that seemed to me a gesture, whilst saying down the midden, dig the midden, etcetera and so on, so that I could reply and he could draw recourse from my response, that yes, I understood, excavating the midden, I repeated, pointing at him. This was how his speech and his ability to gesture took form, first of all in short whispers of sounds, later gaining strength and duration so that what he said anyone in the room could eventually hear. For my part, I no longer had to crouch and listen to follow his words, these words which became sentences that circled around themselves and the themes and ideas that were developed between them and our nocturnal exchange. His thought migrated through the gradual displacement of statements by other statements, with claims repeated but never precisely reiterated. The midden what, returned, just as the midden below, and dropped to the mid, but the context was adjusted, and the phrases accumulated. Every statement became a different version of itself from each cycle. Claims migrated to other points and carried the memories that now occupied his mind, memories which were nothing more than effects, or servicing myths, of the body. These myths had travelled far by now from the noises below and the sound of his choking when not choking, aided no doubt by my own linguistic ministrations by which he was taken to the heights of fabrication and imaginative accomplishment.

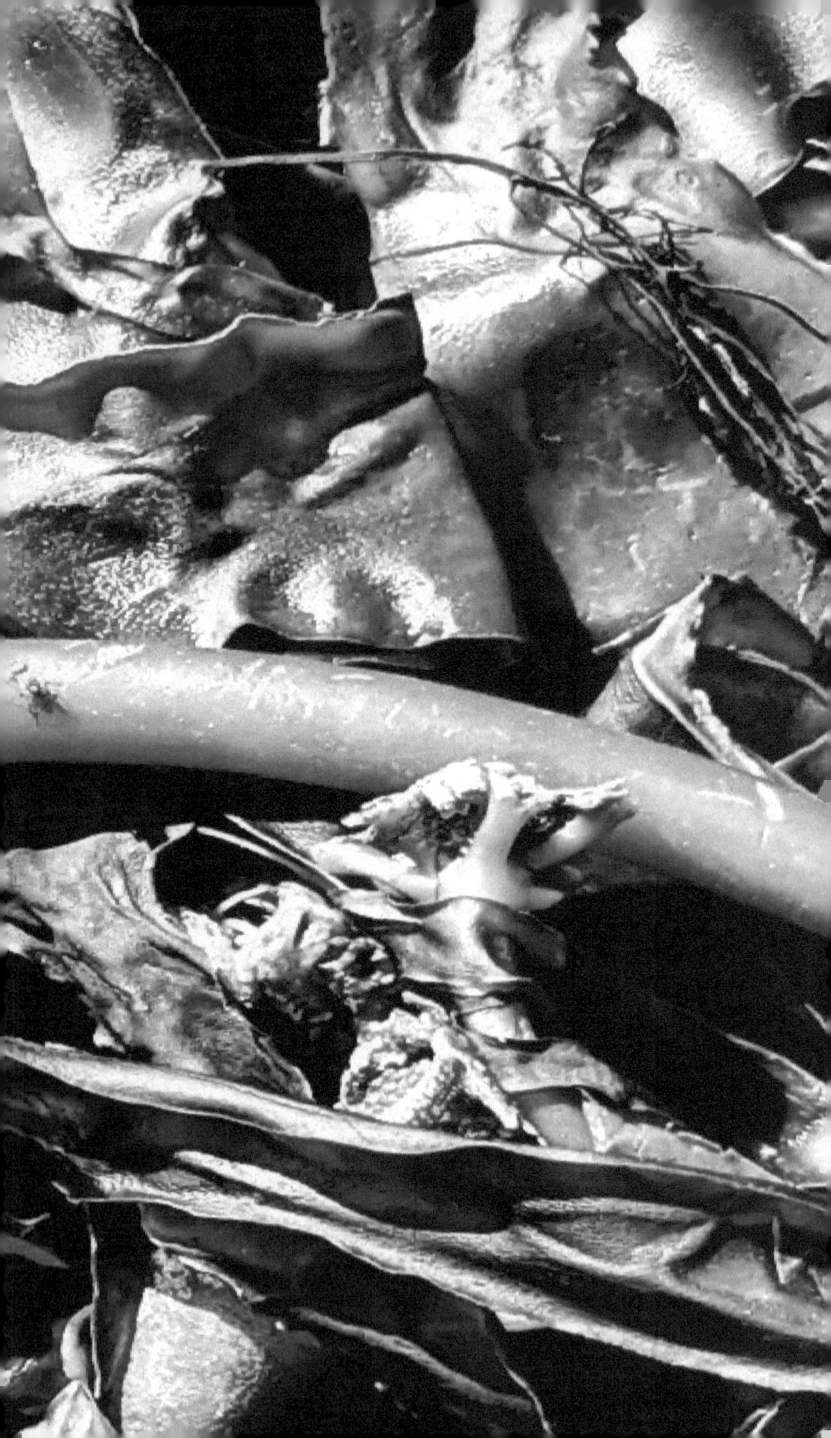

ON THE CONDITIONS OF THE WEED.

Nothing more was said about the midden, about being there, or about digging it, or anything else, for some time. Telling of the weed seemed easier. As he spoke, and as I rested my hand upon him, I could feel the bile move about his body, its cavities fill and release. His words were the consequences of that build up as could be seen in his blood distemper and the fever and the passions that drove his perception and distorted his memory.

The island was surrounded by the weed, so I came to understand, first discovering there was weed all round something, though he gave no form to it. This was not for want of words. His vocabulary was recovered. It was hardly likely he failed to remember the word island, or the words that might describe an island—a great rock emerging from the sea, for instance. Or an indifferent mound. Or a slick. Or a bank. The absence of the word for island in his speech could be explained nonetheless. It was explicable, I told myself. The absence of the word was due to his tendency to misrepresent the reality of the island in his memory of being there, I thought. He repeated that the weed surrounded, or that there was a surround of weed, whereupon what the weed surrounded might be all manner of things in his recollection. He told me the weed enclosed cultures risen and gone, it encapsulated cities from their birth to their destruction, it marked the outer fringes of perception, and the limits of knowledge. He told me about the point at which the extremities of perception become exhausted and venture no further. He said this border is not definite and all was there as the weed did demonstrate. There is no line, he said, either visible or notional but nonetheless consequential as the perception of something gives way to the perception of nothing. There is no obvious place at which that happens, but merely a roughly defined rim, a diminishment marked by the fringes of the weed. Likewise, there is no absolute line where the frontiers of knowledge pass over to their own darkness. As the weed showed by encapsulating both, he said, the border of each is indeterminate. He told me that the weed enclosed birth and death alike within its orbit, although not the birth and death of celestial objects, he confirmed, only those of so-called man, or those of man since men began to call themselves man and before that to his various prototypes. The weed enclosed all human beings who did not yet call themselves men but buried their dead and drove flints into the flesh of animals. The weed contained the last footprints of those who walked with their hands as well as their feet, and then, long after that, the first fires lit by the first nomads, and the first slaughters of neighbouring tribes as well as the first told myth, and the obliteration of myth, the limits ascribed to humanity and the creatures imagined beyond those limits, humanoid figures sought and then obliterated too, strange peoples from the outer fringe with their heads at their feet and their tongues in the sand. The weed encapsulated the first technologies and the latest technological devices, the first gods and the last, the first flesh scraping utensils and the most recent surgical devices, forceps, and clamps. It spanned time, he said. It forced dreams into decisions and decisions into dreams. The weed circumference was the silent cloth that swaddled the infants and shrouded the dead. It took within its orbit cist burials, tomb burials, funeral pyres, and urns for storing human organs that the weed mass regarded with the same abject disinterest as it did the pickle jars of our own time. The weed, he said to me, the weed, he repeated. This weed surrounded the development of art and the layering of the world of human perception. It shrouded the belief systems, the evaluative orders that have risen, atrophied, and died, systems that extended outward limbs that were eventually desiccated by their exposure to contexts they would not assimilate. This weed contained all of that, he said, and more than I can tell, all of it stacked, fallen, piled up. The weed was the only mark of permanence as the world it described was decayed within its perimeters. The weed was a definite border and yet a border that shifted, grew and died and returned and replenished, that retreated and pressed itself and broke off human desire as desires reached within its ambit. Dreams turned inward and became ingrowing and caused abscesses to fester and boil. This weed, a marker of borders, a symbol of persistence, was nonetheless also the signifier of their impermanence, he said. Just as the weed marked the persistence of the unthinkable nothing and declared the necessity of taboo and the haunt of excess, it also fluctuated back and forth against the backdrop of the cliffs, their caverns, and the hills. It was a resolute border and a site of permanent flux. The weed was both certainty—the definition of itself as weed mass—and dysfluency—the destruction of its reaches. The weed was reliable as their limit, but unpredictable too, having its own whims and currents and internal dynamics. The weed, he said again.

I listened attentively at first. His explorations in speech and metaphor impressed me initially as my thoughts became imbricated with his. But then I withdrew my attention and grew tired of his circumlocutions and said, you mean an island, and he nodded, and said, if you wish to call it that, yes. I came to understand, he went on to say, that the weed grew in the shallows profusely and then stopped abruptly as the sea shelf dropped to a greater depth and then to the deeps. The weed surrounded the island as you call it, he said to me, but only the shallower parts, not the deeper, and so this border in weed growth had a definite if not still indeterminate outer limit as well as the inner edge that was marked by the reaches of the tide. This much could be stated even if the limits established by the weed itself were as broad and undecided as its permeable yet at last impenetrable width. The outer edges were evident from inspection across the waves, he said, as were the inner limits within which one might walk and look out across the water to the sea beyond, the great ocean, the void, which is naturally still itself a projection.

He spoke at length. His circumlocutions propelled themselves as he talked of the outer and inner fringes. It seemed to give satisfaction to describe it precisely, and repeatedly, which was the basis of all subsequent imprecision and every halt. He fell back and I wet his lips and fed him paste, and he was relaxed for a while until he started up again, telling me the same, a description that, as it turned back on itself by repetition and return, developed only by gradual adjustment. His circumlocutions lengthened the telling by minutes that acquired weight. This telling of the weed circumference functioned as the motor of his recursive speech and his paralytic fixation. The telling of the weed was the telling of stasis and the telling of determined attention. It propelled his words and his telling without allowing the telling of it to become the telling of something else. After a period of rest the bile would build and with it his distemper. At this point in his recovery, rest was more dangerous than speech, and speech was a remedy to his rest. After a rest period during which his condition worsened, the telling-at-length again took effect and subsequently relaxed him so that he might lie back once more and be fed paste and have his lips wetted. His exhaustion produced the need of rest and the fact of rest returned him to his distemper. And so it was that he suffered again and once over the effects of rest that would propel him back into speech. His telling served as the telling of a self to itself, a telling to not concern itself with what it has seen and perseverate on the weed instead, a telling of weed that was a telling of all things and no particular things. His account of the weed diminished his blood fever, whereas his telling of the midden increased it.

It was in this manner, then, that telling of the weed most entirely closed off the development of his description to a description of things other than weed and so migration to other topics. His trans-millennial account of what the weed enclosed despite the passage of time and the birth and death of civilisations might seem like a telling of other things, yet it was nothing but a cypher directing back to the weed, I knew. When it came about that I suggested the word island, this introduction of the word brought an eventual end to his roving. It simplified his weed perseveration and his weed description and brought its transfer to cogency. The island brought closure or at least simplification to his telling. Giving him land to think with served to prescribe less flexible and more proximate limits to his account of the weed mass and what it contained. His speech was reduced to the topographical scope of a discrete mass, rather than the limits established by a weed mass that functioned as the description of a void-like limit point, a great impassable extremity which extended across time just as it blurred the boundaries of space. My use of the word island to describe what the weed must surely circumnavigate if I understood him rightly also served to relax him, so I decided. He was no longer stuck on describing all things the weed circumnavigated once I offered the concept. He settled on the idea that the weed wrapped the land he now envisaged and accommodated himself to. As he did so, that island took form. It acquired contours and features, then grew a volcanic base, its basalt substance. It emerged from the sea, or perhaps it reached down from its peak to mycelial lavapoints in a moment that might have lasted a geological epoch. He gave his island clear attributes, and was able to describe its edges, its interior, and even its peoples long settled there. When speaking of the weed and what it enclosed, he did not talk any more of the cultures that came and went in all places of the earth, or the evaluative orders that were born and obliterated across time, or the organs that were bottled and the artworks that were conjured and destroyed, all of which the weed once bounded by way of his earlier description. Rather, my patient spoke of the cliffs, and the hills, and the shores. Those peoples he mentioned were merely the dermis of this rock.

The weed, he would tell me, was the agent of my imprisonment. It held the island, you say, he said, and prevented my departure. The weed formed a barrier I could not pass through. This weed must be described exactly now, he went on, so you may get the most telling impression. It stretched from the tidal mark a good distance into the ocean. It was visible as it touched surfaces mottled by the upper fronds and stalks as they lay over themselves there. As you looked across the water it was clearly evident how far the weed lasted, or that it someplace stopped, and the reach of it was considerable. The weed formed a barrier between the island, as you call it, and the open sea, he said, but was a forest when viewed from the seabed. To anyone who dove beneath the waves it hung in the water anchored upon trunks, or hawsers. On land these trunks would be feeble, yet within the aspect of the sea had the strength of pull and flex to suffer the onslaught of currents that tug and warp these oceanic trees into forms and shapes that give a visible aspect to the invisible but relentless necessities of the water. But the weed had limits to its growth, so I gathered, he said, both in terms of the greatest possible length of the plant, which must withstand the currents of the ocean that move the extended fronds back and forth upon their anchorage, but also in terms of the diminishment of light and its effects. We must think, he said, of the origins of the plant, of the seeds of the plant and their purchases and their early life. The weed must begin its growth at the seabed with enough sun, I gather, he said, or it will not develop. That sets limits to where it can begin to grow and hence to the maximum depth of the weed where it does grow. There must be good enough light for it to lengthen upward. At a certain depth it is too dark for the young plant to begin and so seeds that become lodged many fathoms deep never sprout, or if they sprout, they exhaust themselves and die. The origins of these water wandering seeds have never been found, he said. By my understanding no diver has located the frond or the bud or the protuberance that releases these seeds to the ocean. It is a mystery how the weed reproduces and how the young plants come to grow in their position. But as a plant it must have seeds as all plants do, and so we must think of the plant from the perspective of those seeds in their various lodgings on the seabed. This much he had learned from the islanders, indirectly of course, since almost all he knew was by way of observing them.

Nothing about the islanders could be known straight, that is to say, by gaining knowledge or perception from them so that the world they saw and the world they understood might become the world I saw and that I understood, he said. The world I saw would likely never be the world they did see, just as the words I used could never be the words they used. Their words had every place and no place for me in the cosmos they described. They lacked specificity in their application and that is what allowed me to occupy all places and no place in their company. My words specified quite exactly where I was and what I was up to. As a visitor to their island, as you call it, my words had a visitor's approach. Mine sought the lay of the land and the ways of its people.

They specified the location of tracks and where the paths led, which hillocks hid what and where the islanders presently were and where they were going.

They talked constantly when they walked, addressing nobody, least of all themselves. When they were in transit, their words roved unrestrained, not linking to intentions, or implications, never commands. When they were stationary, they were silent. What he learned was gathered from walking behind, training upon their speech and hearing its tones, paces, and its pauses, and from interpreting the intentions of their gestures. The words they used were rarely, if ever, deployed to organise objects. This might be sensible enough if the words were objects themselves, I thought, said he, but I grew tired of that, of thinking all words were objects, and that when they spoke it was just objects acting on other objects. As a concept it allowed me to understand each word as an object is apprehended, and to take their words and treat them as collectable things which carried their own presences and substance and need be nothing more than each intoned moment and gust of breath. Then I grew sick and returned to the idea that words were greater abstractions which derived from still greater abstractions. These words were nonetheless connected to things by some trickery, or unavoidable tether, and this ensured all abstractions were serviceable, which is to say tamed, or reassuringly diminished, and so permanently restrained to the proportions of human living. Which meant all human abstractions were never truly abstract, not really, and I came to think once again that their words were always attached to referents even if those referents were not in view, and that the words they employed were nothing more than gestures tied to organs and these organs had given in to the way of things as they were on the island. The difficulty was how sensate words, or words which were attached to known objects, were mixed in with the many other words that referred, so I thought, to other times or other places, perhaps other ideas of how the world is constituted that the island nonetheless permitted. But it is possible too that these unmoored words said nothing of other worlds and merely accessed minutiae in those moments the islanders lived that my words did not permit me to list.

Naturally I discovered their word for weed and yet even when they said this word meaning weed, or the word I took for it, for they most likely had several, this word generally meant nothing to me to hear it said in any given context. For these weed related mentions to deliver any kind of sense I had to listen out for segments where other sensate words appeared alongside. Most passages made no reasonable impression upon me at all. The positioning of the word meaning weed was often such that it did not correspond even remotely to the weed as I had seen it. Only by listening for passages that did correspond could I learn more of its nature and role in the economies of their perception. By selectively listening and extracting sensible packets of speech, the world of the weed, or the weed for them took form, he said. These passages of utilisable speech were comparatively rare, and so he learnt most from observation still, from seeing them speak and seeing them walk as they passed from place to place. When they abandoned sites, they left glasswork remainders not unlike the fanciful artefacts produced by factory workers of our own land at the end of a shift, but more chaotic, less contrived, and entirely without romance or beauty. They dropped the objects and he picked them up. He took and studied these things and saw them in their light. Here was further evidence of the nature of their perception, he told me, as well as the world they knew and of how they survived that world and the chaos they embraced. Incessant speech and incessant production saved them from barrenness and abjection, confusion and want, he thought. They filled their ears with the reassurance that the noise originated within them. These glass objects too had their function, rendering the universe in dimensions the islanders perceived but could not directly otherwise see. Their remainders were markers of sightless seeing and symbols of industry. Here, again, if not more so, the weed was form-giving even as or precisely because it retained its gesture to formlessness. And it was so in the plainest sense given how the weed was used to make the glass. The objects were related to the weed because the weed was raw material to the object. The relentless production of the object demanded the incessant gathering of the weed. It made sense to him, so he told me, that the weed would be rendered along with everything else in the glass orbs. Actually, he felt the depiction of the weed in glass could supersede speech. Glass renderings were, on the whole, more powerful than their speech approximations at presenting a frieze of the liquid under-realm he imagined. He discovered most of what he knew about the weed, and its conditions of growth, from these objects, or from those of them that depicted weed, or weed-like shapes along their surfaces. Their glass remainders demonstrated how the ocean current interacts with the fronds and the anchors to enliven the weed mass, wherein the best of the objects froze those currents in telling volatilities that gave the solid thing liquid qualities.

As the problem of the weed possessed him, he sought out object remainders depicting the plant. He looked for weed in the glass just as he listened for weed in their speech, and so it was that he found the weed embedded within most of the objects he inspected. The bulk of these containing weed depictions were not instructive, he decided, just as most speech in which there was mention of weed, or merely use of the word for weed, could teach him nothing of the weed he knew or thought he had seen. He inspected each, considered the weed it contained, and decided whether it was an instructive rendering of the weed or if the glass contained fronds across its surfaces that would tell him nothing of its true nature. When weed appeared from these glass renderings in circumstances he could not fathom or recognise, he rejected the object for the next artefact which was inspected in turn. He suspected that proper knowledge of the weed, of the actual weed as he envisaged it, was best known by those who ventured into the weed by diving under. So for a while he followed the very islanders he had seen diving to listen to their speech.

It was not bad supposing, he thought. As they travel into the forest below, the light of the sun diminishes rapidly. This reduction is most likely proportional to each foot descended. The major consequence of diminishment, he told me, was a consequent lack of vitality delivered to the leaves of any plant that should grow there. The quality of the leaves diminishes by the foot too, he said, just as the light lessens and gives way. He told me how he saw them dive in the distance when seen from his vantage on the shore, and surmised from that place how this is what they saw. As they dove, he said, that is what they witnessed, and this is what they knew. I knew it to be their perception, and their knowledge, after considering at length what they had seen and experienced, he said, after watching them surface and climb back over and in to their boats, and after seeing them come ashore and sit and chew and look back out at the waves, a surface that was not long before their ceiling, and knew for sure, as I looked, onlooking, how this was their seeing as if I had seen it too.

With each foot gone downward there is a corresponding lack of vigour in the plant, he repeated. This is what they knew, he said. This reducing vigour, which is also the diminishing possibility of life, issues from a gradual impoverishment of energised particles from the sun. These particles are slowed and eventually halted by the water, so he thought. If they travel further into the deeps it must be by sinking. It is certain, I think, that if the deeps experience the sun, they encounter it only in the form of sunken particles, devoid of their energies and having only their meagre weight for propulsion. The seabed may be covered by these sunken particles, particles of light may even lay thick there from timeless falling, yet there is nothing left of the sun about them. It is a slow and inconsequential falling and it brings no life to the creatures that move about in the darkness. And that, he surmised, must be the reason why the weed did not appear to grow in the very deep waters, beyond thirty fathoms or more, I estimate, he said, or so I understood him. From that point none reached the surfaces of the water. It was not bad supposing to think that at such depths no weed will grow at all. But it was also not bad supposing to decide it differently, and hold that if any weed does grow there, it never reaches the surface and is, moreover, of a sickly growth of limb and frond and stalk due to the lack of light and the pressures of the water. This deeper weed growth can for that reason be discounted as if it does not exist and could not happen.

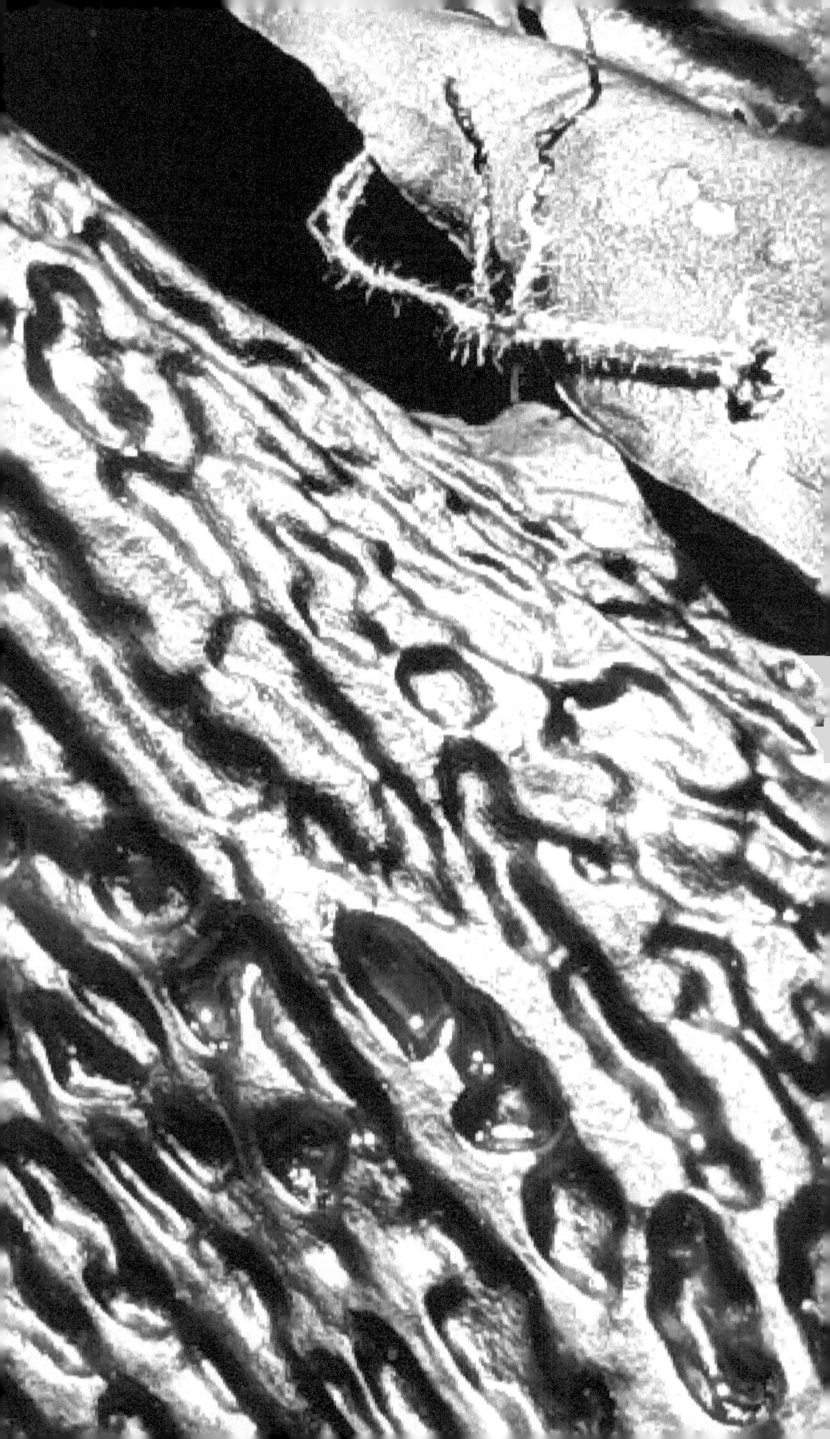

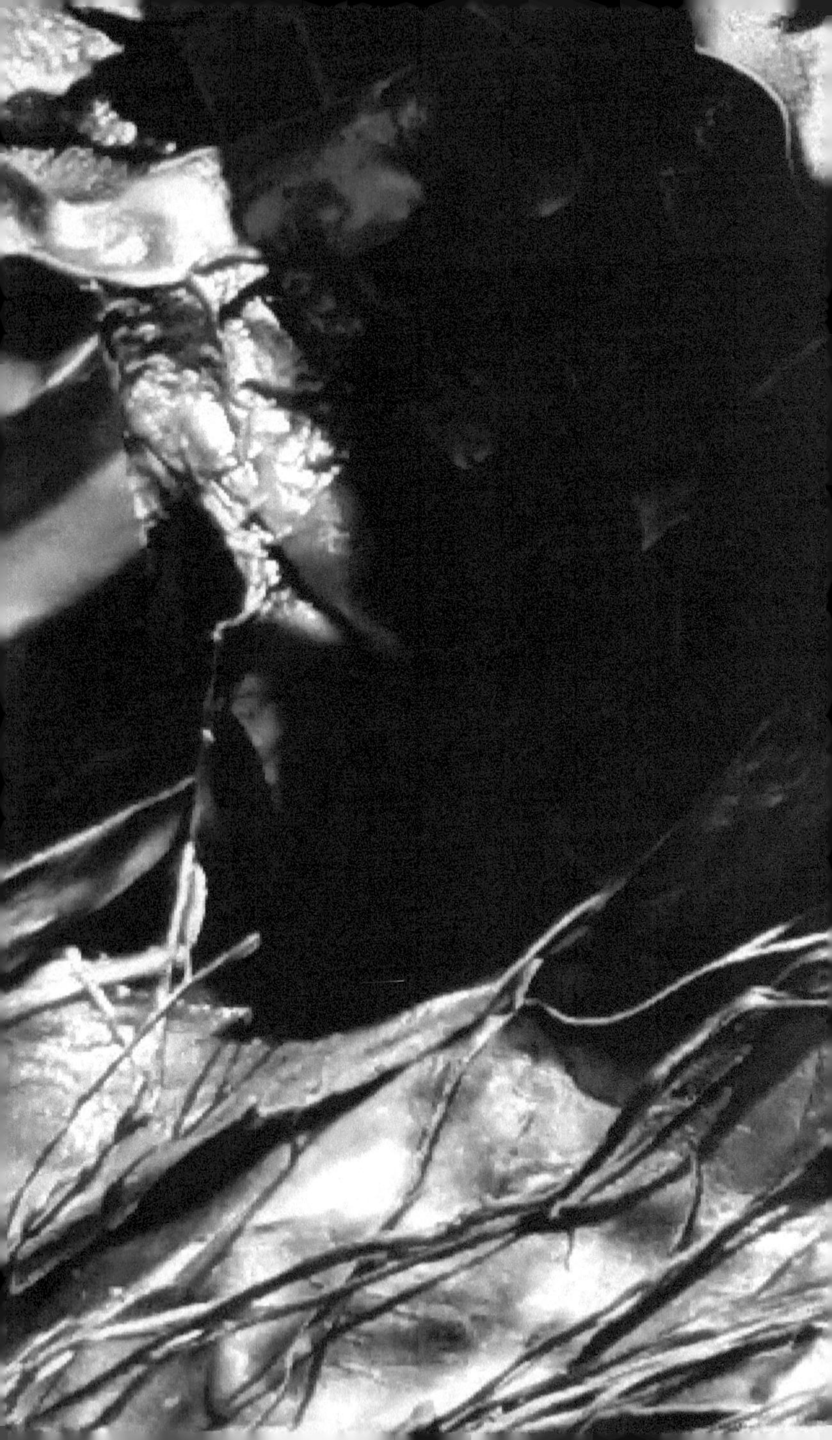

THE WEED HARVEST.

Very small or very sickly things can be ignored if their existence is not worth the effort of noting them down or remarking upon them. This accounts for most existences on earth, and in its seas, he said, or so I understood him. Most existences on earth can be said to hardly exist at all and warrant no attention. And so it might be said that the weed at greater depths hardly exists because the only sun particles that weed growing at such depths will meet are those that sink and carry no further heat. There is no reason not to believe the weed continues to grow in a sickly way much further out and deeper than people can see or dive or dredge. The ocean floor may very well be a sickly growth of weed at its greater depths. Perhaps this is all ocean floors can be. It could be that every ocean floor is covered in this way and there is no ocean floor that is not encumbered by weed. As the fathoms accumulate, their benighted surfaces are still covered with sickly growth. Even where it is entirely dark and not the merest glimmer of a luminescent fish may be found, this sickly growth will continue to sprout. Yet each growth will be an output of the seed alone. It represents the energies of the seeds which bud off from the shallows and are carried across the planet to all recesses and deeps whereupon they germinate and sprout and expire. Each growth will extend for the exact length that the seed allows by way of its stored energies and nutriments. This may all of it be true. But the weed they knew and dove for about the island was not of that sort and grew thickly to the surface. Its existence was worth noting—all should read of it—this existence in weed was its own notation.

The evidence of the weed growth, he said, the sign of the stronger weed, not the weaker, is clear to anyone who walks along the shore where torn up, dead, and decaying trunks litter the beach and rock platforms at the highest tidal point. These were the beaches and the platforms he now described with ease, I noted. He told of a shoreline and by that description established the edges of the island. It gave him the land mass he could focus on and organise his thought around. His speech was still disordered in places. When it worsened, I ignored what he said and merely reminded him of the word island, and with it he would return to cogent recollection. Do you mean on the island, I would say, and his recollection would reorganise, and he would again describe the island and arrange his thought around it. I sat and listened as he spoke, his eyes fixed on me in that small room. I sat and looked at him and noted the stages of his recovery, his intermittent recovery, with its relapses and worsenings. I watched a recovery that mirrored the descent into sickness he suffered on the island and at sea and on the beach here by the hamlet and on the threshold of the house where he was purged and vomited before he came into my care. I came to understand it, and came to know from the route his recovery took as his mind rematerialised and his body strengthened, and as I looked and recorded and waited, only intervening when absolutely necessary, when his mind became disordered and his speech sent itself wandering, to which he replied, yes, the island, on the island as you call it, everything I just described was on the island, he said.

Some trunks arrive on the shores of that island, as you say, having torn their boulders from the seabed. I passed them, he recalled, and attempted to lift the boulders from the beach by the trunk and its anchorage. These trunks might better be described as cables. They were smooth and hard to grip hold of. They taper from the root and a slime exudes on grasping and with the compressing of the sides. It causes the hands to slide along. But with the fronds wrapped about the knuckles some purchase may be gained, although even then, in many cases, I could barely drag them. I would wrap the fronds around my hands and gain purchase on the cables and the roots and heave the assemblage back. I hauled that way, leaning back as I stepped. I leant back so to gather in my mind the extent of the force that will have moved them at highest tide. They did not hardly move. The tide had taken them some leagues but I could not shift them from their position the width of a finger. The force that made them travel exceeded my strength to properly envisage. I would not drag them as the tide dragged them or turn them as the waves pushed them over, although the lesser ones I did manage to rock at their anchorage when the boulder was at a rocking point. These trunks and their fronds were carried upon a storm surge together with their anchorage to the land, I supposed. There they sit, not moved further by wind or toil, and deteriorate in the sun. These stranded examples of oceanic turbulence were, so he told me, clear evidence of the limits placed by the sea and its currents upon the growth of the weed. At some point, he surmised, the weed must reach such a length that its anchorage can no longer be assured and it will be razed from the seabed by the currents of the water. The longest weed of the greatest trunk, of the cable with the safest anchorage, finally becomes vulnerable as the sea floor cannot itself hold them and that floor is wrenched out. Thus the most powerful specimens become weakened, or their anchorage becomes weakened, and the moorage itself sets a natural limit to the weed depth and consequently to the circumference of the weed mass. These, he said, were my understandings of the waters, and this was how I accounted for the outer limits of the weed.

He spent weeks, so he told me, attempting to leave the island. All his efforts failed until the final attempt that bore him across the sea to the small bay and fishing hamlet where he was finally beached unconscious. Every time I attempted to leave, he said, the island would defeat me and the islanders would thwart me. All I did for weeks was attempt my escape and find myself blocked in that effort. The islanders saw me in my abjection as I alternated between begging and demanding their help, and yet did nothing to either discourage or assist. The islanders never directly refused as I pled with them to help me escape, they merely blocked me by their passivity. I commandeered their boats but failed due to their lack of help, never managing to drive each stolen vessel beyond their shallow waters. I could not escape the weed that encircles the island and gathers about the prow, eventually colluding, and bulking, and pulling the vessel back to land with the same force that the oars would propel it outward. These oars, I paddled over and around in shortening and superficial strokes to prevent their own entanglement. I would row outward and eventually be defeated. I would row to the outer edges of the weed where the resistance built until there was no forward progress, only the prospect of labouring to keep in position, from which point I was close enough to see at last patches of sea that were no longer mottled by the upper fronds of the forest below. Here I pushed at the oars until my arms tightened, my muscles spasmed, and I yielded to the pull. This pull took the boat back to the centre of the forest where it sat among the upper branches, all of it as the islanders looked on, and then, assured my boat, their boat, was now at rest, finally ceased looking, their faces turning and their industry resuming about the beach, gathering the weed fronds from their other boats, harvested from below, that they would haul in bales and take away for burning. The boat could not be returned to shore for the same reason of the weed as before when rowing out. And so each boat I left stranded in that zone, swimming back without it.

The bales were assembled by rolling the weed mass together and about itself and by tying it up with the outer trunks that served as ligatures. Each bale was dragged along the sand and shingle to the base of the cliffs. These large bundles—scarce neat enough to be called bales in actual fact—were so big to require leaning in to move them. The islanders lent and hauled each enormous bundle of weed and drove the beach detritus before their feet whilst doing so. The passage of a bale then obliterated all trace of their footwork with its own broad rut. These ruts spanned out to the boats from the winches. At the base of the cliff the ropes from the winches above finished with a hook resembling a butcher's. The islanders on the edge above would draw each bale upward and over to the higher land. Their ropes, a derivative of the weed itself, were lowered for the next bale and the subsequent bale was attached to the hook and drawn, all of which I saw from the sea as I had seen before from the perspective of the land. I saw it all again as I lay in the boat and rested from my defeat before swimming over.

As his account of the weed and his imprisonment by it drew to a close, my patient's speech deteriorated again. He began to scratch and worry at the remainders of the blains on his skin and perseverate over other words and other phrases such as the cliff, the cliff, he would tell me, the winding, the weed fronds, he would say, the winding, the lifting, and then, the bales, the bale takers, and so on. These parts of his account concerning the winding of the fronds into bales, and the lifting of the bales by ropes that were derivative of the weed itself, could only be pieced together after listening to the phrases, and hearing them alongside other phrases, until I assembled the words he attempted into the sentences which became my understanding of his account. There was enough sense in what he said for me to listen and bring together. It was still worth hearing even as his speech deteriorated. Before then, his telling of the weed circumference and the weed imprisonment was clear enough and his sentences followed each another as I heard over and again how the weed circumnavigated, and how the weed contained, and how it reached round and connected its ends and formed an impenetrable mass. That mass enclosed his speech as its descriptive limit and secured his mind upon the anchor points of his account. Subsequent to that his mind was yet again unmoored and his eyes returned to wander. I wet his lips and saw them mutter and decided to let them rest. The liquids I gave after that, delivered by vial, were necessary for the relaxation of his mind which was needful for the relaxation and recovery of his body.

The instruction of sleep is one of the greatest and most easily administered prescriptions in the doctor's possession. It is of a different order to the kind of rest had in wakefulness, the rest that caused his condition to worsen. As he lay back exhausted from his account of the weed mass, his distemper returned. The resting that he managed during his wakeful hours was harmful to his condition, whereas the rest had in sleep, the kind of sleep I administered, a dreamless sleep, was precisely the kind of sleep he required. Sleep is after all the means by which the organism repairs itself. It is the organism's defence against the activity of wakefulness. The waking state is necessary to survival—all the higher organisms must wake—but the waking state is also a killing state. This because the condition of existing in a wakeful state wears at the organism and deteriorates and eventually kills it. Organisms must wake in order to exist. Existence in the higher organisms is, basically speaking, wakefulness. But the necessity of being in a state of wakefulness is also why the organism dies, for the condition of being awake kills it, though not before the waking state actively deteriorates it, as anyone struggling to sleep must already be able to sense in their fibres.

Against wakefulness, which I consider to be the condition of existence, the sleeping state may be understood as its under-condition. I consider wakefulness to be the condition, whereas sleep is the under-condition. The condition of existence, which is wakefulness, cannot be understood without reckoning with its under-condition, which is the return of sleep. This because sleep is the actual living state, or is the state that maintains the organism for the killing state and prevents that state from accomplishing itself. The wasting caused by circumambient bodies, the rubs of bodies and the collisions of bodies, may be staved off entirely during sleep, and the wasting effects of the body on itself may be slowed as the active principle and self-moving reflexes of the organs such as the gut and the heart are lessened in amplitude and frequency. The heart by beating, and the gut by contracting along, are each themselves organs that deteriorate the rest of the organism, and might be viewed, somewhat against reason, as deleterious to its health. They too produce collisions, and these collisions are what wear it down.

The mechanics of the mind are similarly productive of frictions. The condition of existence for the mind, its wakefulness, is also, and in a similar way, the killing state of the mind. The mind deteriorates when it is awake, and if it remains awake too long, the killing state takes over. This is why the mind requires its under-condition, the state of sleep, in order for the mind to continue to exist on its return to wakefulness. But the under-condition, natural sleep, is necessarily imperfect, and that is why the mind of the organism deteriorates during its lifespan until it is finally ready to die, either with the remainder of the organism or in advance of it. Hence the advantages of the doctor's prescription and the dangers of the profession. The doctor may administer the remedy, but the doctor suffers in his profession because the killing state of the mind is worsened by thinking, and the doctor's professional life is nothing, after all, but a thinking life. The doctor's life is marked by the onslaught of overmuch thinking which is why doctors suffer in their work and will often prescribe unnatural sleep to themselves as well as their patients. To work as a doctor is to spend more time than would be naturally spent in a killing state of mind, that is to say, in a state of thinking. The profession is a noble profession for no other reason than this— the doctor must suffer more than the patient from this killing state of mind. Actually, the doctor spends more time in this killing state than any other person, I would say, due to the hazards of the profession. Which is why doctors administer unnatural sleep to themselves with such avidity because they have spent much longer than any other in a killing state of mind. Here the wasting caused by circumambient words, the rubs of words and the condition of words, may be staved off by entirely dreamless sleep, the sleep of soporifics, which the exhaustion of ideas, the death of conscience, and the absence of curiosity, will also approximate. Those who exhaust their ideas already in their youth, who pass into adulthood with an underdeveloped conscience, and who have managed to resist every lure against their habitual lack of curiosity, have managed to protect themselves as no doctor ever could, even with the most advanced soporific. In the higher organisms, almost all agitations may be solved, at least temporarily, by the use of a potent soporific. If I meet a patient in a state of distress, I will merely administer a sleeping potion until the period of distress is completed.

I have often been pressed upon this point as I leave each patient in a condition that, from a non-professional point of view, seems worse than before I arrived. Upon my departure the closest or near closest family member will clutch my arm and ask, effectively, if not so plainly, why their loved one is worsened by my treatment and not bettered by it, to which I reply that the worsening is only apparent and they should not trust their eyes. When this does not satisfy them to let me go, I offer my professional explanation, or tell it so they listen. As bodies are impaired and wasted in wakefulness, I tell them, they must be repaired and restored in sleep. You wish for an unhealthy state. You hope I would leave your beloved in a more wakeful condition, but this could be fatal. Wakefulness is basically productive of the tendencies that diminish, wear away, and point towards annihilation, whereas sleep pauses that decay, and may even afford some repair to faculties and organs that were destroyed during periods of consciousness. You want to exchange words with your beloved, yet to bring your mother or your father, your son or your daughter, your husband or your wife, into a state of consciousness might well kill them. You would have me kill your father, or your mother, your wife, or your friend. This is what your consternation and your disappointment amount to. You think they are closer to death because I have visited, but this is your misperception. The conscious state is the deleterious state, whereas the state of deep sleep is only mistakenly approximated to death. Wishing to see your beloved awake is like wishing their end. But over and again and despite my best efforts to enlighten, each patient of mine who no longer moves is falsely thought to be close to death. You falsely think and you persist in thinking that I have, by my presence, and by my treatment, done your beloved a disfavour. You do not understand as I understand that the state of deep sleep is the only guarantee against swift and certain death. This has been shown beyond doubt, I tell them if they press me further. I know this, I say, as experiments with inmates at prisons have seen. Prisoners have been made to die by the simple deprivation of sleep, that is to say, from an excess of wakefulness. I have heard of extensive experiments in this field. These experiments have been proven by rigorous redoing, according to the maxim that if an experiment can be repeated multiple times, its findings are irrefutable and the experiment itself was a decent one. Well, I have seen these irrefutable findings. Those conducting these experiments have scarcely believed their results and have been compelled to repeat the test from the full propulsion of their disbelief and not merely their scientific rigour and so check they were not mistaken. They have done so by a scientifically sanctioned infliction of reason akin to rubbing the eyes into the realisation of seeing. As prison guards and prison wardens can testify, merely keeping awake will be sufficient to kill. Sleep is the remedy to wakefulness, I tell the family as they assemble and as they begin to complain that my unnatural sleep is not a remedy but a worsening. Wakefulness is not to be desired in this case, I say. It damages the organism. This is why the body cycles between wakefulness and sleep. Think on it, I recommend. When that rhythm is interrupted by excessive stimuli, it must be imposed artificially. I have imposed on your beloved a condition that only resembles death because you do not realise how much wakefulness is the actual condition of death and not sleep. And so it continues until I am sure they are sufficiently worn over by hearing me talk.

With his sleep administered I took my opportunity for the sea air which, in small quantities, can invigorate the soul and not overly enliven it as it did now for me with mine, so I felt, moderately stirred upon the shore by the hamlet. I walked across the bay and away from the stench of the small dock, its boats, and their over-repaired nets, to where the timbers of the coble still lay and where his clothing which had fallen off as he was disentangled could still be inspected. My interrogation of these remaining cloth fragments revealed little to me but the fact he had once been clothed with reasonable modesty, but not entirely without expense, indicating he was not of the poorer type in wealth and outlook—a fact I could already tell from his speech—neither was he of the higher class of person, a fact again of his speech, although it may also have been a fact of these fragments alone. These were, of course, only rudimentary conclusions. My speculations were derived from limited evidence but they did at least confirm what I was told about his discovery here amid the wreckage of the coble. The weed that by their account had entangled him to it and saved him and so on was nonetheless absent. I tried to find this fabled weed in and about the nearby rockpools where it might have been swept. Yet here was merely the usual weed, the typical weed, the unsurprising weed of these minor places in which I found two sea slugs engaged in the activity of crawling over and being crawled over. Such is their own life habit.

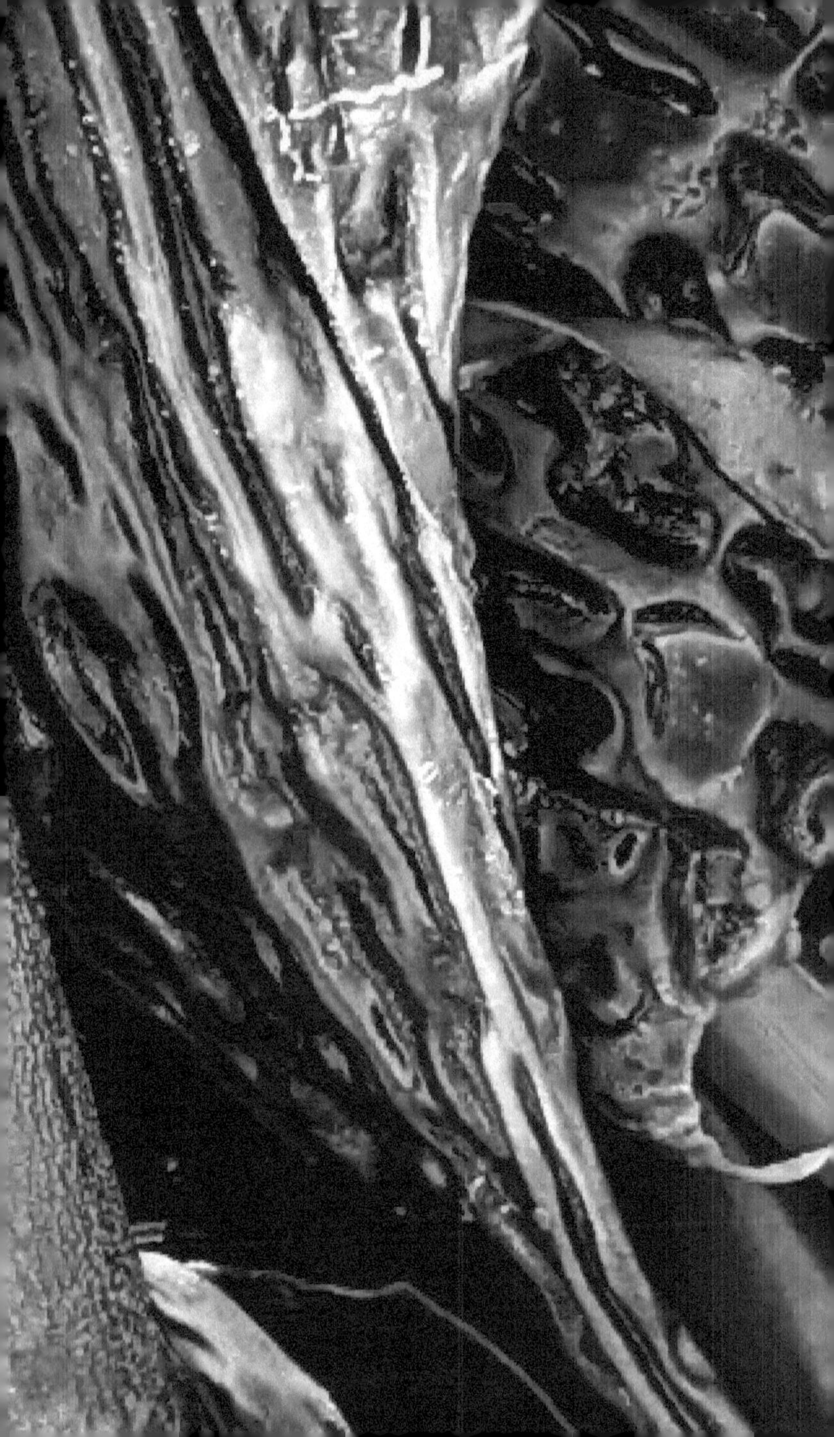

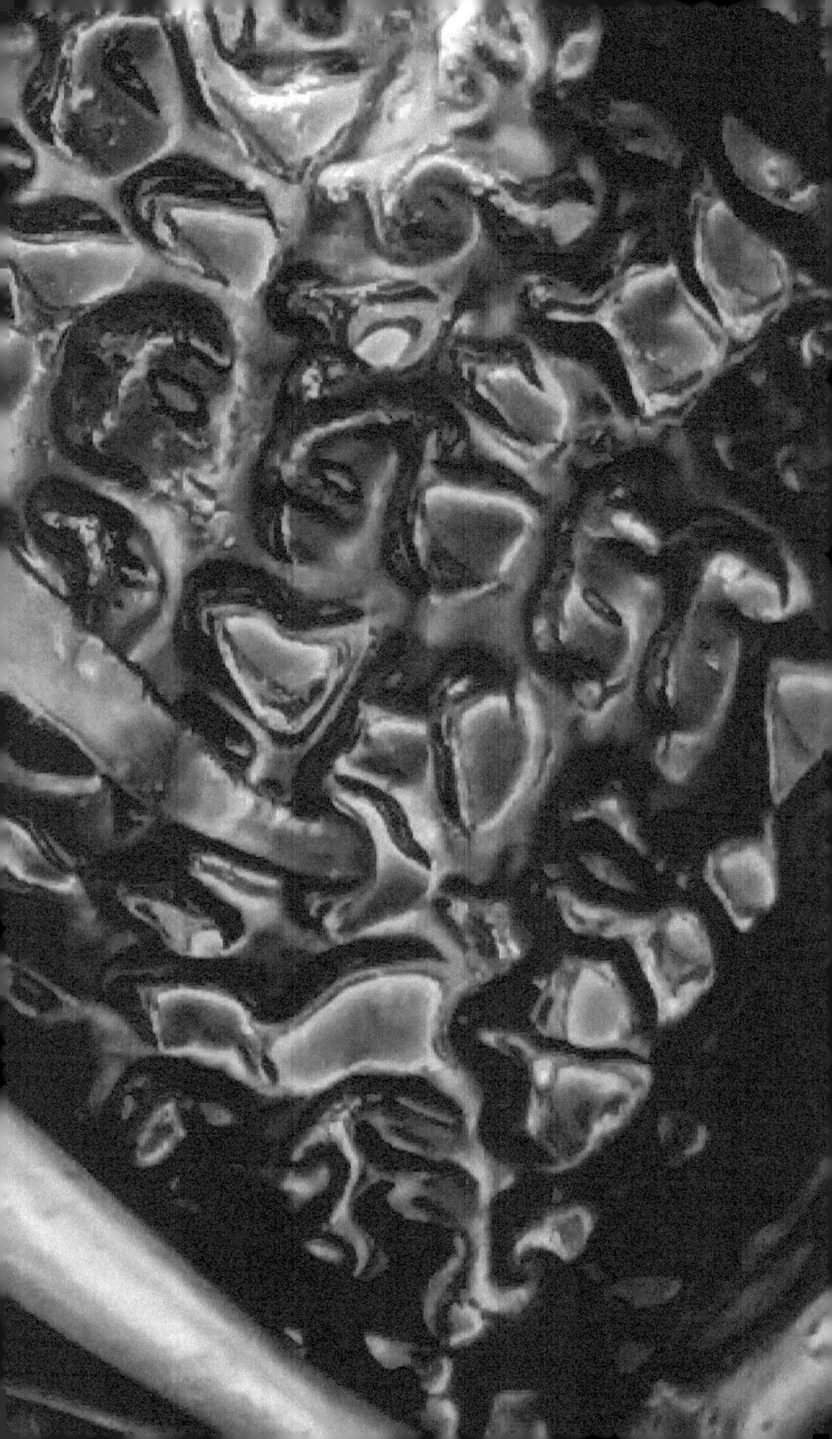

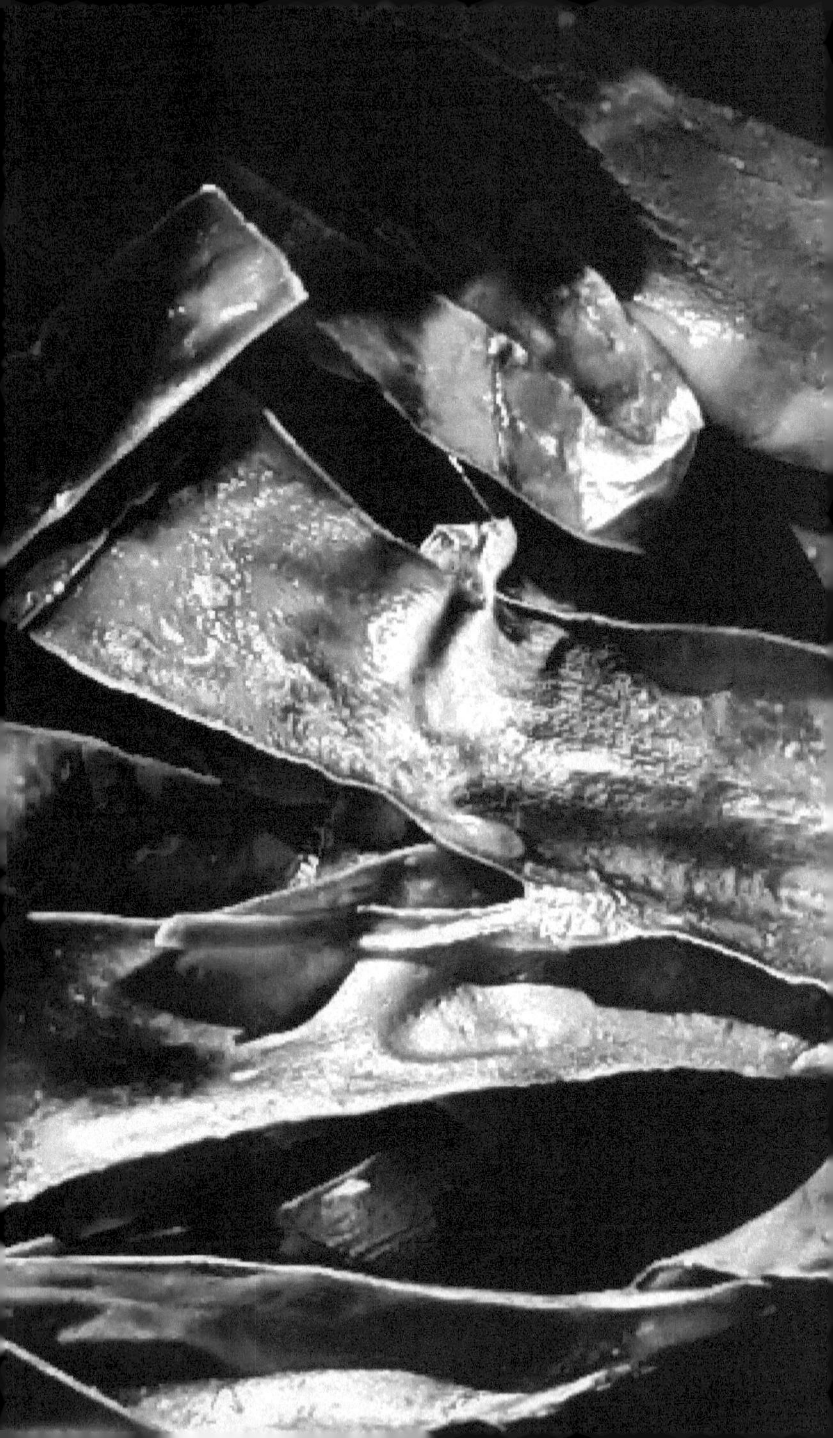

THE ISLANDERS AFTER THE REPORT.

I found the report close to our encampment, left by the track the islanders presently used. They passed us each day and we remarked upon it. My employer and I would talk about their coming before continuing with our writing the report he dictated and that I scribed. When we had nothing else to talk about, we would discuss it. We would say, look here how the islanders pass us by, look how closely they come now to our encampment, look how their route has changed, look here, and listen to that, their route is now right by our sleeping place and when we sleep their feet very nearly tread our heads.

We heard them approach, speaking incessantly, and heard them pass and then walk on. To leave the report there, a few paces from our encampment, was a deliberate act. It was sure to see as soon as I saw the report by the track that my employer had placed it there for them to find. By the time I found it, the report was open, and some of the pages were strewn about and others missing. My employer most probably left it there shortly before we went to the shore. When I found the report lying like that, strewn about, I stood reckoning with the consequences, realising the situation I was now in, standing there, close enough to hear my employer still at the fire, rattling the kettle on its chain. As he rattled the chain, I thought about his decision which could only be a calculated decision, a decision that was taken for its effects. Holding a page, I shrunk backwards from our sleeping place. I crouched down as he lifted the lid on the kettle—I could hear that clear enough—and as he poked the embers with his foot. Walking my feet gently I then turned about and when about hard into the ground. I put so much distance between us as the island allowed.

In the days that followed he stalked the slopes of the island for sight of me and I fled from one part to another and lay in holes where I found them. At times I heard his stick tapping and approaching and fled again, listening for him, fleeing him, and so travelling from one makeshift camp to the next. The moment I discovered the report had been read, when I saw pages of it fallen in the rut, I knew this was the end of my stay and the end of my time under his instruction. I would have to find a way out because of what the report would bring. I could see no immediate impact, my patient said, whispering still and holding my arm, but was sure how reading the report would change them. It would make them unpredictable. Before the islanders read the report, they were indifferent. We walked up to them, and watched them, and they scarcely seemed to see us as we saw them walk and heard their speech. As I fled him, and when I saw the islanders, I thought about their reading. I moved from one place to the next and wondered about that, about if those I encountered had seen it, first of all, and then about if they had digested it. Or, if those I met with had not seen it, whether they had spoken it to those who had. I knew that some had seen it and I was convinced they had digested it. I thought about them seeing it and then about them digesting it. I looked at them straight and thought, you have not only seen the report, you have taken it into your consciousness. I slept where I stopped, and never with them. I could not sleep as I slept before. When they looked at me, they did so with eyes that had seen his words as he inscribed them, as he wrote them, as he had me write them down whilst he walked round me in loops. They looked me and saw more than they did before. This reading of the report, of their character and their making and the materials they were made of, surely changed them, I thought. I saw how it changed them as they looked at me. As I looked at them, I knew that they were changed. You are changed, I decided. You are entirely changed and cannot be trusted even though you are exactly as I remember. Having read the report you have been influenced by the report and you have been moved internally by it without doubt even if this change is imperceptible. Even if you look just as you looked before you have been changed irrevocably by reading his account of your existence, I felt. Their words were not fixed like his, so when they read the pages, they encountered the order of his words which was the order of his thought. The islanders had naturally heard me speak just as they heard him speak, and so they were familiar to some extent with our words and our tendency to organise and pinpoint what we saw. They had sensed that tendency in our speech even if they had not commented on it, or responded to our words, or reacted to us at all as we spoke in their presence. We suspected at first our perception meant nothing to them as they listened, just as their words meant nothing to me as I sought to understand them in their particulars. These words could not be followed in terms of their intentions. Their words tied them to no place and followed through with no consequences. The islanders did not act upon their words. The words they spoke had no greater significance and bore almost no relation to their habits. These habits were hardly fixed themselves, even if they were observable and for short times even predictable. The weed itself, harvested by going under the water and gathering and rolling in bales and by the hoisting of bales, all in ways that gradually adjusted, so that the going under was done a little differently, and the bales took different forms, and the hoisting occurred at different rates and angles until they ceased hoisting entirely and dragged the weed along the shore to a point where the cliff dropped and the weed could be pulled inland to where it was burnt.

The burning itself was a site of continual flux—vast fields of activity that shifted as pyres were abandoned for new burning grounds and glasshouses left for replacements. The first I saw were set in a valley by a stream, each squat and made of stone. They were abandoned for glasshouses on a slope which were themselves left for glasshouses situated on a plateau where the earth was pitted by depressions filled with water. Above these, subsequent houses were placed and the molten glass dropped into the water during the process of manufacture. As the water boiled and deteriorated, other houses were built on neighbouring pools so that fresh pieces might be created. These were the particular pieces of glass I inspected at that point. They were long and irregular, bulbous at the end, formed during the extreme tightening of molten bits that hit the pool and cool into shapes that had a toughness glass will otherwise not boast. These houses strutted over pools were then abandoned for houses built directly on the shore, on the sand that was their chief material, the main material for the making of glass, to which they would reach from holes in the floor and grasp up for the melting, and then these shore-sited glasshouses were left for glasshouses on stilts above the tidal rock pools into which the molten glass would again drop, and so it went on. The island was full of abandoned houses from previous works. I encountered them as I walked across it, avoiding my employer just as I avoided the islanders. These were the ruins I slept in.

The islanders continued to speak and incessantly so, and they continued to migrate across the island, gathering the weed, burning it, and making glass objects from the ash and the sand they took from the beaches. The report my employer dictated extended in its descriptions from the gathering back to the creation of the artifacts. It covered all of their other attributes and slow migrations, or those we observed, including the manner of their talking and the structure of their speech. Such a report must have its impact, I thought. It will surely be felt. There is no doubt. It will cast them to themselves differently and make them think otherwise about how they lived and what they did and how they looked, so that they could no longer merely shift from one habit to the next just as they moved from one part of the island to another. The islanders were now conscious of their migration and the transitioning they underwent, all which had occurred until then as a simple result of their living so we thought. His report would drive them into themselves.

As my employer paced in circles and as I inscribed his descriptions at their centre, I set down how they looked from the perspective of his gaze, the perspective that would locate them and pinpoint them in our descriptions. As they read this report, the report which he left for them to read, they were most likely rent by it. Reading our report introduced the idea of the islanders as such. They were not conscious in this way of ours before that. Before they read the report, they could not be aware of their own definition in an amongst our thinking. There was no other way of explaining how they spoke. His report would destroy the facility they once had to rove and meander, or if the report did not destroy that facility, it would mean they could only rove and meander in full consciousness that this is what they were doing. They would have to choose to rove, they would have to intend to meander. Their wandering had to become deliberate. It would need to be their aim to do so, to stray, to become aimless. They would make this wandering habit the basis of their understanding of what they did, which means they would no longer truly wander, or stray, or rove. They would hold it up as a personal or a collective characteristic. We wander, they might simply say or simply think, and that simplicity would reduce everything they were to what they now said they were. If they did not change at all after reading the report—for I could detect no difference—it was because they decided to live unchanged. This was a decision they repeatedly made, and so was a decision they might cease making at any moment.

I came to this conclusion, my patient said, in a moment of distinct clarity. He was fully present, he came to full presence as he explained this to me there in the room. And I knew from this point, he went on, that the islanders had chosen to live unchanged, and this was why they looked unchanged. They chose to live unchanged just as they chose to speak unchanged. They chose to migrate from word to word just as they migrated before they read the report. In short, their world revolved around making the same choices and thinking that their making choices is what made them what they were. They opted to retain their speech as it was, only this speech was now a decided, intentional, and communicative act, and not a natural act that had nothing to do with communication, not as we understood it. It was their decision to speak expansively after reading my employer's report of their expansive speech. That speech was not propelled by their words and their impulses. It was enacted as imitation, in memory of. They chose to imitate how they had once spoken just as we had heard them speak. If they sounded as they sounded before they read the report, this was only because they made their own speech as they recalled it, or as they knew it subsequent to our description. This was their chosen nature. And the perversity of that decision to be as they were, to continue as they had once been, only made their aspect more terrible to me. They meandered in speech not because their speech meandered of its own accord. Their speech, their ability to meander, was ruined by their reading of the report. It was ruined because they were, they had to now be conscious of it. Reading the report made them know of how they spoke and how they meandered, he went on. Before they read the report, they spoke without fully knowing the form of their speech. Having read the report, they knew its form, a form that my employer had given shape to by reflecting upon it and by describing it. He gave it form by having me inscribe it. My employer gave it form as he paced around me at the camp and tapped his stick to the logic of his dictation. They would now be able to reflect upon their words with exacting correctness. With his encouragement they saw their words before themselves and they felt their words appear. They could no longer speak without thinking on their descriptions and noticing their perambulations as I reflected on mine. They would speak sightful of how they might be again received, in recollection of how they were deciphered and inscribed, because they now returned to themselves as they spoke. Their speech, as my employer wrote, had been heedless. It had taken upon itself a rendering of realities they could never know, just as their speech occasionally rendered those realities they would have known, so I thought, as my employer wrote, as we heard them talk and watched them move. Now they could know nothing more of all that, and their world was restricted to their intentions.

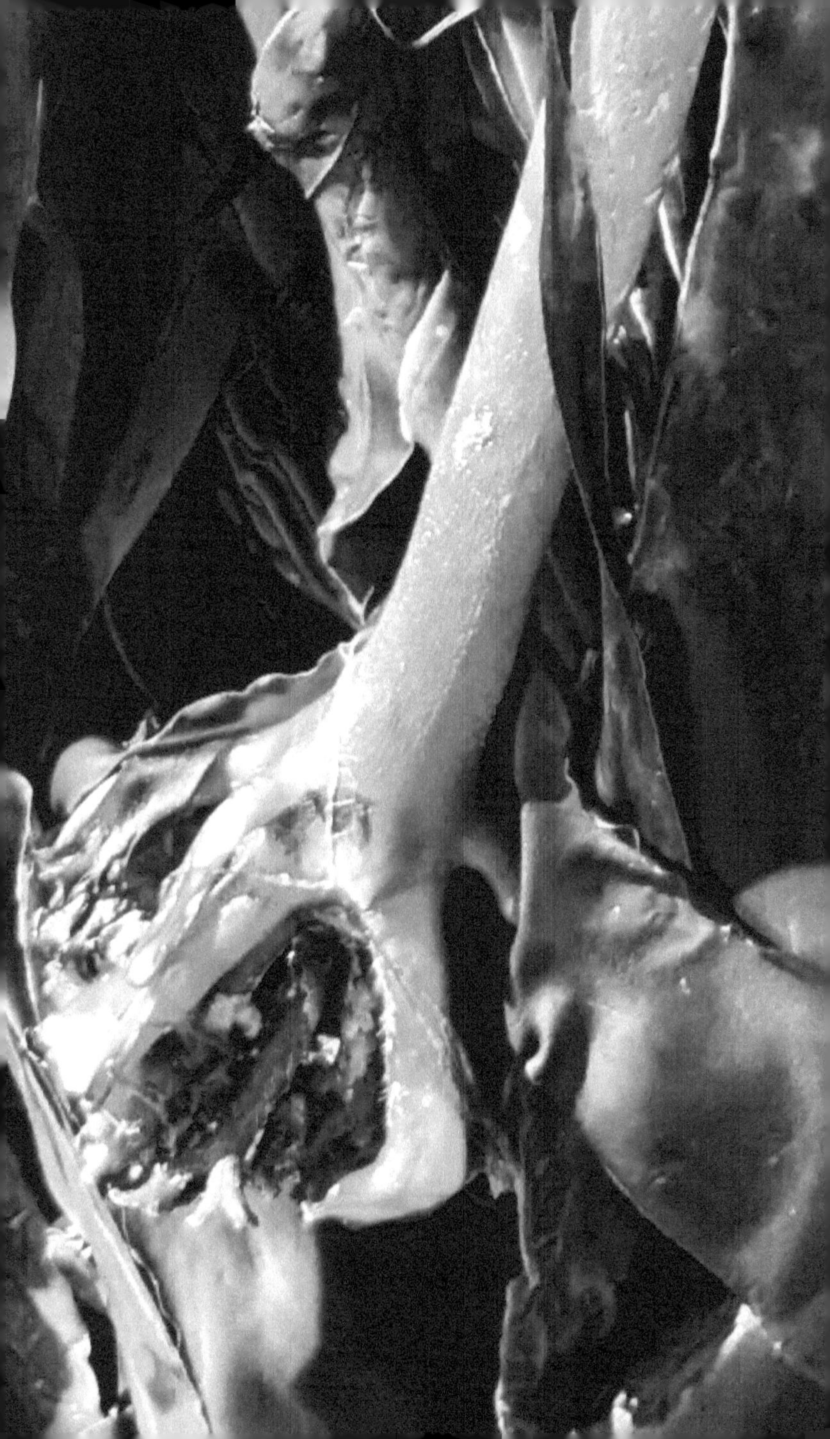

THE SEAT OF THE HOUSE.

Our assignment was this. To record what the islanders did and what they said. We went to the island to report to the main house about the work, condition, and habits of its inhabitants. This because the overseer would not leave, had not left for years, and had no reliable means of knowing what his subjects were up to as they worked his lands—or neglected them, and as they looked after his animals—or ate them up, and as they tended his industries—or forgot the command to do so. He had long suspected his servants, or those who brought him reports, were falsifiers and liars. Their reports contradicted one another and themselves and besides which disfigured the land he knew, but he could not risk driving these last messengers away. He listened to them deliver their news and sat in his great seat, entirely silent, knowing that most if not all of what he had heard was a distortion if not an outright fabrication.

The seat was at the centre of the house in a room which might be described as a hall, though it had all the qualities of a lobby. It gave way to the rest of the house by a host of doors, these leading to the rooms and passages that went to the other parts of the building and finally to its boundary. The overseer did not walk to those edges. I am not sure he left his seat. From that place nothing of the edges could be seen, only the intervening rooms and passages that served as his first walls, a labyrinth that took his vision into their chambers and exhausted his sight and his perception before it could reach the further borders of his dwelling spot. He would not travel to the edges of the house and open the shutters and look to confirm his suspicion and his memory. The outer wall was protected by a second interior barrier. This was the first skin before the outer, and it served as a final restraint. If the overseer wandered into the halls and passages of his house and found himself near its edges, that first boundary would remind him of the proximity of the outer and he would turn about and into the passages leading from the inner skin which directed the wanderer back toward the regions of the middle. This directing backwards by the design of the house mitigated against further encounters with the edge, we thought. The inner propulsion mechanism, or the design of the house and its chambers, ensured all further approaches for that span of time were ruled out. If the overseer wandered, his wandering tended inwards.

The house was easy to locate because of the paths that led to it from the midden. The midden itself was easy to find because of the tracks that led to it from all parts of the island. These were trod by those few islanders who no longer gathered the weed, bundled it up, burnt it, and turned it to glass. They left their occupations and walked to the midden when they became heavy and began to show. Some later walked from the midden to the house and this was where they became trapped. When the islanders became heavy like that, they clutched their bellies and walked off without talking. The other islanders continued with their activities, seemingly oblivious.

The pains of labour adjusted their language. No islander would wish to be around this use of words nor be responsible for burdening others with their directness. It caused the pregnant islanders to leave and live apart until their speech was repaired. They sat above the gaping crack in the rock and gave birth there. They brought their children to crawl and then to stand against the threat of the midden and watched their children respond to the demands of the world and become linguistically competent as if these demands had no purchase upon them. These little islanders were in their intermediate phase, not yet opened to the life of the island, such as it was, with its wanderings, the gathering of weed, and the peregrinations of its glass workshops—ways of life, of speech, of production that the islanders followed and whose practices changed in the following of them. The little islanders tottered about on the rock escarpment and fell easily and made noises that resounded from the surrounding cliffs. We sat and watched them clamber below us. Their mothers had to work hard to prevent them from rolling off the escarpment or into the midden. They survived by eating the small plants that grew in the cracks between the rocks and stones. And then the islanders eventually left with their children and returned to the gathering of weed, the pyres, the glasshouses. We saw them return and when they did so the mothers walked like giants. When the mothers came with their children and went among the other islanders, they seemed taller to us all. When they gathered weed, they carried larger bundles. When they dove beneath the sea they were gone without air for much longer. When they talked their speech reached new regions of description. And when they took molten glass from the furnace, they produced objects of impossible complexity that were painful to look at.

All except those whose infants who did not become linguistically competent, who still attached words to things and made demands of the world by way of them. When their children were big enough to be condemned, their makers walked off with those infants and did so without a word or a glance at the others to mark their departure. They were not dejected or despairing. They walked with the simple decision of their predicament. We found them living within the house, gathering where the floors were level. If they attempted to leave, they were driven backward by the internal architectures of the building. For as we ourselves discovered from the draw it effectuated, the compulsion inwards that held the overseer in place afflicted his visitors too. As we subsequently attempted to leave, we came up against the same inner prohibitions. Like the overseer and those before us, our passage tended inwards even as we forced our way outwards. Following our audience with the overseer, we found ourselves reacting to the first skin as the overseer may once himself have reacted. We could not make our way to the second membrane, the outer wall, and its door. This was our first and only encounter with the first skin of the house from the perspective of its inside. We approached it that time and then turned about and found ourselves led backwards upon ourselves. There would not be a second encounter with the first skin because the passages conspired against our coming back.

The two of us arrived at the seat at the centre of the house. The overseer raised his head and said, Get out. We attempted to do so but returned again. That caused him to raise his head a second time and command us to leave. Our passage through the house continued in this way with voyages through its halls and corridors that would finally end back at the seat of the house and from which we would again be repelled as the overseer raised his head. After a while his agitation grew. He no longer said but shouted at us to leave. We arrived back at the chamber where he sat and his head was already raised. Get out of my house, he cried as we came. So we hastened across the chamber to another of its doors that might lead, so we hoped, to the edges of his first dominion and its outside.

At some point we changed our approach to the problem of leaving and began to follow the servants.

They were easily tracked through the house as they went about their business within its labyrinth and we kept behind them as they walked and as they carried objects from one part of the house to the next. We went along as they did their work and fulfilled whatever duties they had, including the lighting and relighting of the lamps affixed to the walls, the replenishment of their oil, and the winding of wicks. We tracked along as they walked from lamp to lamp and were still following when this duty took them past the trapped islanders who were generally huddled in the darker corners. We discovered how at intervals the islanders stirred themselves into motion, crawled outward and raided the house for food which they digested back in their sitting spots, doing everything they did to no particular end beyond the living of their confinement. Unlike the other islanders, including the ones who returned from the midden, they did not talk when they moved but were silent as usual when they sat. Their infants did speak, and we saw that the sound they made was difficult for their makers to hear. We rarely met the same trapped group a second time. Most looked up, appeared struck by our walking past, and then gazed inward again. The servants themselves were not noticed by them.

Trailing was easy when we were in those parts of the house near the centre and in the region of the overseer. We kept sufficiently near to his servants to know which way a servant went but not so close that our following would cause them to stop. The servants never turned at first when we followed, nor did they seem to listen, and so a few steps behind would do. But their behaviour changed as we travelled further from the interior parts and came closer to what we thought were the outer regions of the house. The servants quickened their pace in these regions and became furtive. They tended to turn more often and would do it fast to see who was behind them. When they saw us, they stopped, and if we did not retreat they stood for as long as we remained. Our only option upon them seeing us was to walk away and become lost again in the corridors of the house.

These servants were professional dissemblers, we came t see, and the overseer had good reason not to trust them. He knew from memory how the land they described bore no relation to the place he remembered from the seat of his house, the extent of its property, its industries, its dependents, their ways and their enslavements to him. It was of course possible that the place he remembered might be no longer the place his servants visited. The place of his dominion as it appeared in his memory might not be what they actually saw and walked through and then turned into the substance of their reports. For years he sent his servants out and requested an accurate description of his land and they returned with stories of his house, his dominion, he simply did not recognise. He sent commands, orders, and the servants went away to issue them. But those servants returned without confirming what they had done or verifying what they had seen in a manner he would accept.

I was too careful to ask, but my patient addressed the question in any case. The occasion of our being there, at the house, at the seat of the overseer, he said, is not easy to account for, by which I mean our being at the house and our being at the island. I know what my employer told me, and I know what the overseer told me after that. There were two accounts. One travelled with us to the island, the other met us when we finally arrived at the house.

Our invitation presented itself in a dream, my emploer said. I could not accept this explanation but was bound to him and the story he told by way of it. I followed in full doubt about his account of the invitation he received. I heard him tell himself about his dream as if that telling it to himself would make it true. I listened as he told me how a dream called him as if a dream was sufficient reason to act and it was reasonable to act upon a dream. I heard him tell himself how his dream-induced invitation assured he would find the island without a map, or a sea chart, or a compass, and that the island could not be found by way of these things in any case. Or that if anyone did reach the island by way of a map, or a sea chart, or a compass, these devices would only be accidental accomplices to the voyage. I heard him tell himself the island could only be reached and so too the overseer could only be approached at the seat of his house by way of the world as it had been imagined. He said he would only get there by the propulsion of his mind, or the lower part of that mind of his, and if the higher part had anything to do with it, those regions would be subordinate to the lower, and so on. And this is what accounted for the mirk, he added. The invitation assured him, so he said, that the circumference of the earth would yield to the description that his recollection gave, should it be needed. He said that his dream was perfectly specific on this point. The earth, he said, will submit to my imagination. The world will be made navigable by it. Or more adequately put, the world will yield itself up to my imagination. It will re-form itself where necessary to fit with the lower regions of my mind. The world, he said, will fall and rise by what my mind may conjure. Seas might fill regions not touched by water for a thousand years. Mountains shall recede into the crust and plains will erupt with freshly extruded yet weather beaten rock, if I imagine it. He told me how the way to the island already appeared in the dream, in full detail, and his imagination was already rendering the island itself quite precisely before he saw it. He said none of this should surprise anyone given how his imagination was always enslaved to his limits, and so the island, and our route to it, would be nothing unusual in the scheme of things. But he said little or nothing about what precisely it was he saw by the mind's eye, so to speak, and how what he saw managed to anticipate the overseer's request, or receive that request, it was not clear which. All of this my employer told me with his usual sluggish precision. The ambulant percussion of his words filled the space we then occupied, as they always did, leaving no outer recesses for my own to occupy.

And yet it struck me even then, my patient added, how my employer had none of the enthusiasm of a dreamer who has just woken and wishes to tell every detail before the dream is lost. He did not tell me of his dream with this kind of enthusiastic haste, with the characteristic form, the immediate candour of a compulsive retelling, a mode of speech driven out of the mouth before the precipice, before the prospect of a swift forgetting. And so it was that we journeyed to the island, to the seat of the overseer, with no ready story for how that journey was contrived nor detail of its particulars. No sure or testable notion of which oceans we would cross and in what directions of the compass or the stars, and what land masses we would need to stride across and perhaps eventually stumble over. The only specifics my employer announced were that he could hear, And can you not also hear, he said, the sound of a valley just beyond our seeing. I can hear it filling with brackish water, soon enough it will be a fjord, or perhaps a delta. Or how there was a rumble, and could I not detect it too, the sound of a massif just over the horizon. I can hear the massif raising itself from the crust, he said. It was all as his thought gave permission to think. We were called to the house, to the seat of his perception. We were called in this way to occupy it and subsequently became trapped within it.

For his sake, the overseer at the middle said our calling arrived in a bottle shaped like a boat, that it was built in his private glasshouse and sent from the river of the seat of his house—the seat of his perception—to the sea. I doubted that too. By the time we arrived, the river under his house was dried up entirely.

He said as we arrived, I am glad you got my message. I have waited so long for you to get my message and now here you are. You will see how I sent it, he said, indicating the hatch under his great seat. This hatch leads to the river that went to the sea. This was how I dropped my message to you. The river is lately dried and so I have ceased sending my messages to the world. Which of them did you receive, he said to us, because I sent many and so describe it to me, tell me exactly how the bottle was shaped, give me a precise description of its design and I will know which message you responded to, who you answered, which house you made for, and the land you anticipated from my description of it. My employer paused to consider his request and then told him that the bottle he sent was figurative, that it had a dreamlike quality about it, to which the overseer replied, ah yes, I know the one, and was satisfied.

Write me a report of the island, the overseer said, so I my know the extent of my dominion again. We stood before him, at the centre of his house, and took his words as they were given. We will write your report, my employer said, so you may know the extent of your dominion again. And I will assist in the writing of it, I confirmed as the overseer looked from my employer to me.

My employer prepared me for the visit by telling, Tell nohing of what we have seen already. He told me to be silent before the overseer, to give minimal responses when directly asked, and never at all mention the midden or speak of our excavations there. He told me this repeatedly as we made our way to the house. Do not mention the midden, he said. Whatever you say make no mention of that, he repeated. Do not use the word midden or any other word that may give it away. As we walked over to the house following the track, he told me again to say nothing to the overseer about the midden or anything else, and I almost stopped hearing him say it. Best not to say anything at all, he said. Say nothing unless he addresses you, he continued, and if he does, just tell him back what he most expects to hear. Repeat what he tells you in your reply, my employer said, and do not tell him anything beyond that. Take his words and give them back as if they were your own. Make sure these words are only ever his, he cautioned.

We already suspected the overseer had no way of seeing us outside and so we had not hurried to visit. We had been on the island for several weeks before we finally went to the house in which we were subsequently trapped. There is no reason to hurry over to the house, my employer said. We can delay our visit, he said to me. And so it was my employer and I stood looking at the house soon after we arrived, and he turned to me, and said, there is no need to go there yet. Already when the house was at some distance he suggested we would probably not visit it after all that day. We looked across the shoulder of the island to the house as it stood, alone, the earth around it bare and compacted from where the paths converged. When we were still some distance from the building and a long way yet from the convergence of tracks into paths into earth that were its gathering approaches, my employer turned to me and said, I am not sure if we need to go in right now. He cannot see us. He has no idea we have arrived. If his servants tell him, he will not trust them. He has no way of hearing of our coming, or if he hears of it, he will not believe any such report that makes its way to him. Let us walk to the house and decide, my employer told me, but I suspect we will not go in.

We eventually stood looking at the walls of the house, the single door, and the bricked-up windows. The structure was raised on its foundations to a considerable height. I noticed that the foundation walls contained seepage holes and that these holes were large ovals. They were the sort a retaining wall might have to let out moisture, except these holes greatly exceeded that purpose in their diameters. They were large enough for an infant, I remember thinking. Each hole would pass an infant. A very small child would be able to pass right through them, I thought to myself. A long ladder led to the threshold of the single door, the entrance, this door black against the white quarried stone of the building. We stood at the ladder and I stayed it with one hand and held our luggage with the other, waiting for the command to go up. I stood there waiting in the silence of the shoulder of the island. No, we will not go in, he cannot see us, my employer said. I have decided, he told me, we will not enter the house until we are left with no other option.

Having spent weeks on the island we finally went there and climbed inside but only after we exhausted our supplies and came at last to need the house we had so diligently avoided. Do not mention the weeks, my employer told me as we walked along the track. Betray no knowledge of his dominion, he said. Do not tell him where we have walked and what we have seen. We have already observed more than enough for the writing of his report, as you know, he said to me. But as far as the overseer is concerned, we have just arrived and must have no knowledge of his island.

You will need supplies the overseer said from his great seat. My employer replied that yes we would need supplies and thanked him for his suggestion. It will take you time to record all aspects of my dominion and for that you will need a large quantity of food and so on the overseer told us and my employer agreed that all aspects of his dominion could only be rendered fully if we took the necessary time, perhaps weeks, to produce our exacting description, our definitive description, the description of the island that would lay out each and every aspect of his land before him. And yes, we would need plenty of food and so on, he added. Take the time you need, the overseer said, and take what you need from the rooms of my house. Take food and materials and do not ask my servants, do not trust them with it, just gather what you require. We will do as you say and gather what you describe, my employer replied. We shall take only what we need so that we can return with your report. I will be waiting, he said, and we left the overseer seated there, blinded beyond the limits of his chamber or those rooms and passages he perhaps occasionally visited.

As we left and began to make our way through the house of the overseer, my employer turned to me and said—Now back to the camp, we will complete the report at the camp.

ON LEAVING THE HOUSE.

It seemed we could not make our way out and could not return to the overseer who was shrill at the sight of our coming back. We thought about the hatch below his seat and wondered if we could lift it with the chair pushed aside. Each time we returned to the chamber at the centre of his labyrinth we looked first at the hatch and then at the overseer who was still sitting there blocking it. We would make our way through that door in the floor if we could lift it and crawl the course of the old riverbed that was culverted by the house. That hatch led to the river and the river led to the sea, the overseer had told us so, and so we could take the same route as the water once did. If we could move his seat a little and raise the hatch, we might lower ourselves down, or climb down, or drop through the hole. We might gladly drop a good distance. We would travel by climbing down or falling in and thereby escape the house of the overseer. We would grasp the iron ring, haul the thing over, and lower ourselves into the riverbed. This is what we would do, we said. But the overseer did not leave his seat or even stand when we returned by the ways of the house that permanently delivered us to his chamber. We arrived having failed once again to leave, and the overseer shouted at us once more as he sat and continued to sit right down upon what had surely become our only way out of the house. He shouted, and we hastened to another door that led away from his chamber, knowing the only route was beneath him.

The problem, my employer came to think and came to tell me, is that we are influenced by the architecture of the house. As we sat in the house, unable to leave, he told me this. We cannot leave, he told me, sitting back. He decided to tell me long after we found ourselves to be stranded there, telling me as we rested, just as we had leant back so often against the walls. We cannot leave, he said, because the architecture has influenced how we think. As soon as you and I climbed the ladder to the threshold of its door we submitted ourselves to its arrangement. The islanders did exactly as we did, he told me, but they did so willingly. As they dragged themselves up that ladder and as they dragged their children up behind them and reached under the door to open it, they knew exactly what they were doing. When we made our way up that same ladder, we had no idea of what we were doing. We did not have the advantage that the islanders had of knowing what was coming. We could not know that the architecture of the house would come to occupy our minds and prevent us from leaving. We went to the overseer to answer our summons. We did not go to the house to see the house. The house was incidental. If we went to the house with knowledge of it, we only went to the house in order to answer his invitation, which made the house not so much a house as an instrument in our reply. We had no particular interest in the house itself, he said. We merely went to see the overseer and for that the house was a means only and not an aim in itself. This detail is crucial, he added, my patient told me, if we are ever going to leave. We must realise, he said, that we did not come to see the house and so we have no interest in the house. To us the house was a mere route to seeing the overseer and answering his request, he told me, and we must not leave sight of that. To the islanders the house was not a route to something else but the destination they needed. To them the architecture of the house answered their failure to introduce the island to their children. They went to the house because their children were not receptive to the midden experience, in which not falling to the midden was their first basic lesson, a lesson they repeatedly failed to learn as their makers prevented them from tripping into the fissure or held them off from rolling over the escarpment. They went to the house when it was decided that their children could not exist on the rock escarpment and so could not exist on the island. These children had to be brought to the house, the only building of its kind, he said. Once it was determined they would not live on the island because they would sooner roll off its cliffs or into its fissures than walk across it, they were brought to live here. Once their makers realised that their infants were resolute about falling in and were fully inclined to this decisive act, and even if saved would remain decisive in all other respects, they had no other option but to make for the house. This house was the only place on the island that their infants could be let upon to inhabit. That is what the house meant to their makers, to those who birthed them and saw them grow to consciousness. The house was the only home, the only place, for anyone who was even remotely resolute in their outlook to exist. To us it meant nothing, and we must remember that. It means everything to us now, I know, he said. But once it meant nothing. We did not think of our existence or our non-existence in relation to the house. When we approached the house it was merely the route to the overseer. It had no independent significance and we did not anticipate the house in any other terms but as the place where the overseer would be found. So know that again, he told me. Know that it meant nothing to us. We did not anticipate the house at all of its own standing, we only anticipated the overseer who called us here. When we made the ascent we did not realise that the ladder itself was already submission to the seat of its inwardness. We could not know, as the islanders knew, that each rung took us into the architecture of his mind and would leave us trapped there, would have us live there within its confines and with no chance of leaving. As we raised ourselves upon its rungs, we came to inhabit its restraints. Our first step on that ladder was decisive, my employer said. As we stepped onto that ladder, we submitted to him. We were driven from our own perception to his perception, my employer told me. We were forced to accept as a condition of entry that not obeying his architecture would be fatal. As we held onto the rungs of that ladder and reached its highest points we submitted to the mechanical principles of our predicament and made our first concession to the mechanics of the house. From the heights of that ladder to the rocks below, it was a fatal drop. We knew that as we climbed. The islanders knew it too as they dragged their infants up and over. Anyone who climbed that ladder knew it was a fatal drop, or if not a fatal drop a near-fatal drop, a fall that could not be suffered without permanent damage. Anyone climbing the ladder would grip it tightly to avoid that fatal drop or that near-fatal drop and ascend it slowly and without excessive movement to keep the ladder in its position. But the islanders knew the greater significance of their ascent. They dragged their children up that ladder because they needed to release them to the mechanics of the house. They sought those mechanics for the sake of their infants, submitting themselves to the mathematical principles of its architecture even though it would restrain them too and cause them to become withered. It would be a life worse than the life they had just abandoned at the escarpment yet one in which their infants could live. It is not so very unusual for mothers to wither in favour of their children—some would say this is what motherhood amounts to—but these islanders withered more badly than most. When you clawed your fingers under the front door of the house to open it, he said to me, you submitted yourself to the logic of this place, to the design of the house, just as the islanders submitted, he said, but you had no understanding of that decision. I submitted myself to it in turn, he admitted, as you, on the threshold, pulled me over the top of the ladder and into the house. Do you remember when you pulled me over that threshold, because when you did that, you had me submit to the logic of the house. You hauled me into the house just as you hauled me into its logic. We looked back from that threshold across the land, I recall. I spent some time looking before you closed the door. If we had known, we would have looked for longer. We saw the pyres as they burnt across the further points, and then we turned from those expanses and submitted ourselves to the corridors. The islanders did not look back, they knew what they were leaving, but still, they did not look back. We looked back and had no knowledge of it, not knowing what we were leaving, that we were leaving for so long. That ladder and our ascent was how we acceded to the design. We gave ourselves to the design of the house as we went up that ladder. Our entry was on the condition of our acceding to it. And so the problem we are presented with here, he continued, is one of separation from the conditions of its architecture which condition our thought. We can still escape, he assured me, because we never willingly submitted to our imprisonment. We unknowingly imprisoned ourselves, and now that we know what we have done we can escape what we unknowingly did. If we cannot exit this building because it influences our direction and turns us inward, we must refuse its direction by thinking ourselves out of it. The only way we can leave is by separating our perception from the perception of our surroundings, my employer said. He suggested we imagine ourselves elsewhere, yet our memory of alternative artifices was not sufficient to overpower our experience of the walls, the angles, the lines, and the confines of our present surroundings. My employer recalled his family tomb, and how he had crept into it as a boy hoping to see where his family slept—as his family put it—and then crept out of it by a different route because his uncle came looking. He recalled the route he took, so he told me. I am recalling the route I took, he said, so that the route I took in my memory of it will overcome my perception of this house. As he told me that I closed my eyes and held onto the tails of his coat. I am leaving the tomb, he told me. I am leaving the tomb, he said as we walked through the house of the overseer. I am leaving the tomb just as I left the tomb when I was a boy and my uncle came looking. My uncle is descending the steps, and I am retreating to the back of the tomb where a crack is formed in the wall. The earth has subsided from the bank beyond that wall. It has given way at the base of the cemetery. Soon the feet of its incumbents will be poking out of that bank. For now it has only revealed the edges of the family vault. The river has undercut the bank and has undercut the cemetery. The family vault has become a house. We are emerging, he told me. We are small enough to emerge. We are thin as I once was when I was a boy, thin as a boy, we have a child's thinness and we will pass through walls because of it. Our family sleeps now with a breeze from the river. Hold the end of my coat as we walk, he said. We are leaving the tomb where my family sleep. We are leaving the tomb, he repeated, and my uncle cannot follow. We are leaving the tomb where my family sleep, he declared again, until finally his words were cut short by the call to Get out of my house that greeted us as we returned to the chamber.

His second suggestion was the better one. Since we cannot imagine ourselves outside of the house, my employer told me, we must change our relationship to its architecture while we are still in it. We must resist its hold upon us, refuse the demands it makes. When the walls and the corridors lead us to think in one way, we must think in the other direction. We must perceive our environment in such a manner that directly opposes how this place would have us see it. Left will become right, up will be down. The lure of each corridor and the lure of its architecture must become the repulsion of each corridor and the repulsion of its principles. It must fail to lead us one way and take us the other instead. Everything we believe must become its other. Our perception is at fault, is driven to error. Anything we utter is mistaken. We can only say what comes second. Our memories are false and so we must work to misremember them. We can only leave this house if we oppose every thought we have with its counterthought, making sure, he added, that each counterthought is not so much thought as thought-revulsion. We must drive all thoughts to their inverse with ruthless imprecision, he said. We must become ruthless to ourselves because our thought is the symptom of our environment. Our memories have been employed by this house to misdirect our path. Everything we thought we knew has been set by its architecture to mislead us.

These were again words written at pace against the closure of memory. When his head fell back, I took up my journal and made these collections of his speech. As he rested his head, the last thing he said is that he could not remember how they came to think contrary thoughts and how they came to misremember their memories and misperceive their surroundings. All I remember, my patient told me, is that we found ourselves at the base of the ladder. The door was closed up at its top. The walls of the house faced us and we faced them back determined that the house was nothing to us now, this house was nothing to us, or if it was not quite nothing, it was the contrary to everything we had experienced within it.

He woke from his rest and interrupted my writing of what he said. Before I had finished my account he was awake and telling me again that he had no memory of leaving the house. But when they looked at it from the end of the ladder, they could see the house had been peeled back as a torn apart orange, or a fig. The house, he said, was turned back on itself. The outer walls were folded and curled and the inner voids and corridors were bent and distorted so that the flesh of the house was torn, the fabric of the building rent and exposed to the desiccating sun. We could not see its occupants. The overseer had not been turned out of his chamber by the unfolding but no room was intact or shaded from the glare. Our inversion of the house was accomplished. And then, soon enough, the house stood as it did before, the windows bricked up, the ladder at its base, the interior hidden from the glare. We will now write the report, my employer said. Let us return to the camp where we will write it. I will dictate my report of the things we have seen and I will tell the extent of his dominion.

As I recall, when I looked down at the first page of the report my employer had me write, I saw that the words I wrote curled over themselves as the fibres of the page raised up and curled back in turn. The ink erupted from the inkwell and the nib of the pen peeled open. The skin of my fingers inverted to the ligaments and turned the fleshy innards over to the light. The skin then folded back to its former position, the inkwell ceased its turbulence, and the fibres of the page were reconnected. With these fibres the words themselves were returned to their form. His dictation stopped and the report was complete.

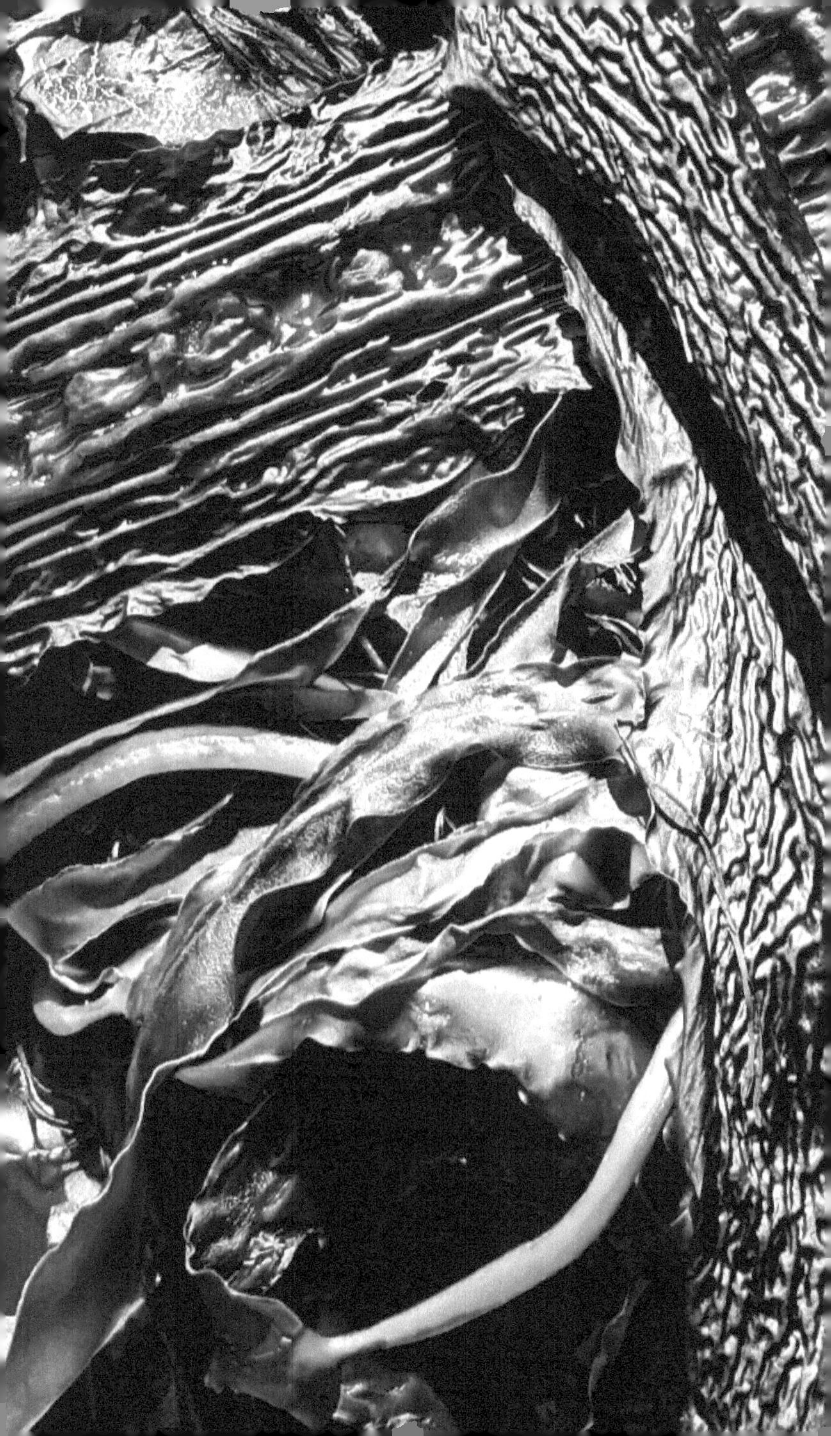

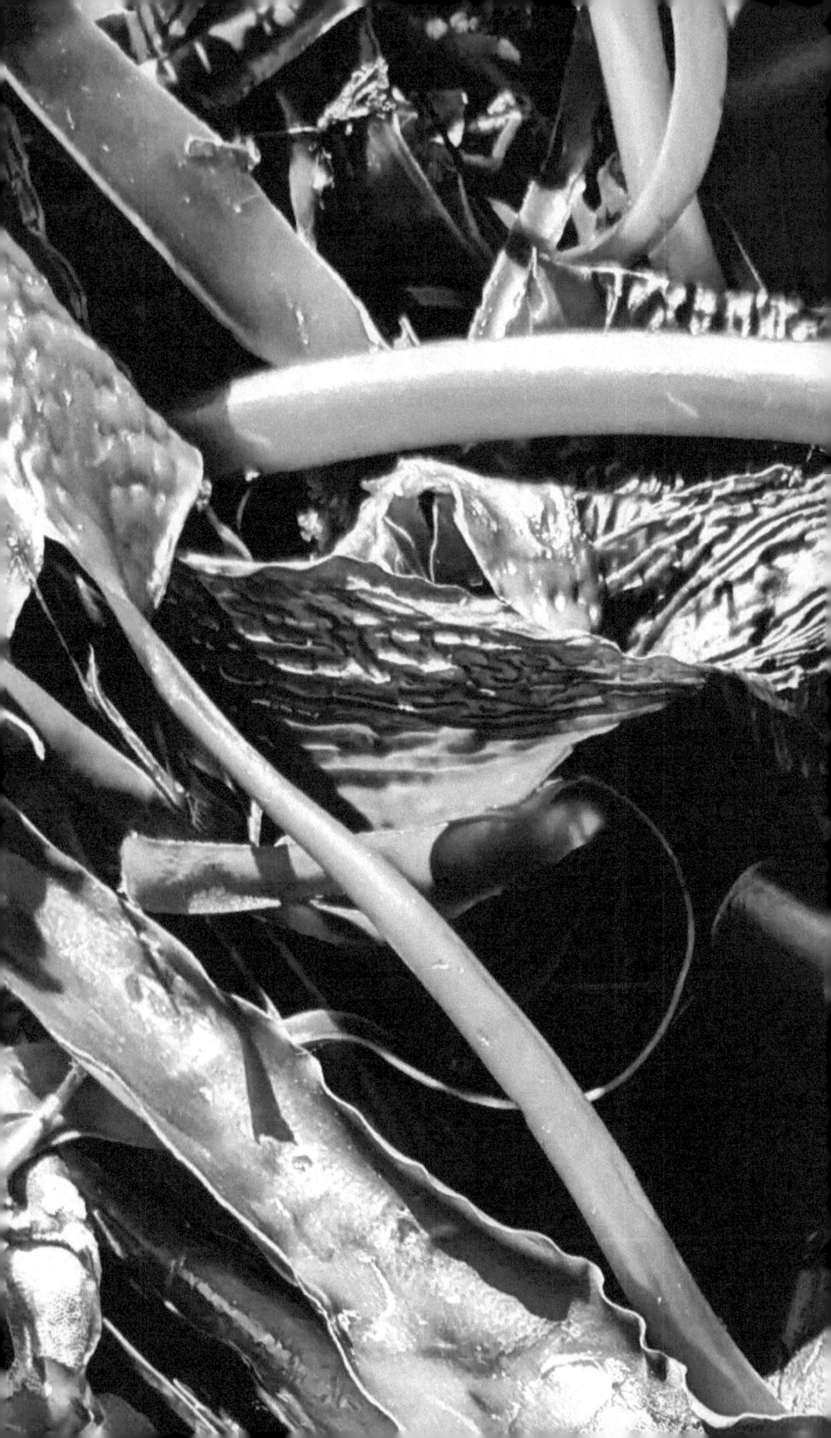

More Details Concerning the Weed.

I went to my bag to administer another soporific and by the time I returned the man was fallen asleep. This sleep would do him no good nor restoration. I examined his skin and then shook his arm till he woke.

In most cases it is unwise to disturb the animal functions during sleep. It is likely the interruption will cause a blockage, or a non-returnable deployment in the nourishment of the damaged parts that sleep sets out to remedy. The body recruits the blood and in that state of recruitment this gathering of the blood is aborted just as it is fully enlivened and ready for release. Most people will think nothing of shaking another from their sleep not knowing it can be fatal or at least damaging by degrees. The accumulated effects of being shaken from sleep must not be underestimated. Those who live in circumstances where they must be shaken to fully wake tend to live shorter lives and die from multiple points, although the exact mechanism of that shortening remains unclear and I am left with only the rudiments. A mechanism might be imagined where the waking would kill, or diminish, by the following pathway—The delivery of nourishment by the blood, which is prepared and gradually released from the moment of sleep arriving, is left unfinished due to premature wakening. This may build the pressure of nourishing juices at their borders and cause inner lesions. I have known of patients who died as they woke, as if they were woken at the wrong moment. I have seen their loved ones wake them and do so against my advice, and soon enough the patient wakes, suffers a debilitating attack, and dies. In this present case the danger of dreaming for my patient was nonetheless greater, and so, weighing up the damage of one against the damage of the other, I decided upon the damage of waking that was the lesser of the two, and shook his arm to recall him. His sleep would not restore the tone of his nervous fibres, so I had to remove him from his natural sleeping state. His was, in his current condition, a dangerous sleep. I had no choice but to prevent it. I frequently advise against natural sleep. I council against drowsiness and prescribe against it. Although more typically my advice relates to digestion, and not to the adverse effects of dreaming. I am rarely confronted with the problem of dreaming as a reason for not sleeping, but I am reasonably familiar with it. In a typical sleep state, the healthy state of sleep, dreaming may be endured if some of the time spent asleep is not spent dreaming.

The body repairs itself when the mind dreams, and both repair themselves when the dreaming stops. Dreams are unavoidable in natural sleep—they are the residual effects of waking stimulations and cannot be prevented. These dreams are, in most cases, not excessively damaging. They are merely a regrettable affliction of the animal functions. In some rare cases dreams of such force take hold that they undermine the restorative action of sleep. I have seen their effects when left unchecked. These may lead to a loss of sense and appetite, as well as extreme sensitivity to the sun or other lit objects, eventually the inability to distinguish day and night and terror before movement, resulting in facial features that become contorted and eventually fixed, and in the overall withdrawal of the organism from stimuli. His dreams were by far too livid in their effects and undid all the work of rest that he might otherwise have benefitted from. And so only soporific sleep was permissible. I prescribe the exact same sleep for digestive problems too and for entirely different reasons. I administer sleep to my patients when ordinary sleep is plagued by digestion. The problem is this. A natural, restorative sleep will not occur when it should, which is when the organism is quiet and so in the necessary position for the restorative effects of rest. I wait for the right moment when digestion is at a lull, and I administer the soporific. I ensure that the patient remains awake until that point and does not fall into natural sleep, which under these circumstances would be harmful. I demand abstinence in the consumption of food and wait for the alimentary system to quieten. I hold my ear to the stomach or listen by a tube and when the stomach falls quiet, and the gut ceases to convulse, I am ready with the sleeping potion. Most sleep disturbances are because of the stomach. The stomach is over-stuffed, and the load of it exacts its levy on the remainder of the organism. Congested with food and crudities, it will not allow sufficient rest to the surrounding organs and eventually conveys its tumult to the seat of perception. This seat suffers like all the organs, each of which suffers in turn, those neighbouring the stomach being worst afflicted, those at one remove less so, and then those further on to a lesser extent again, but all still burdened by the stomach to some degree. This causes sleep to be ineffective, if not positively destructive, so that sleep conspires with wakefulness in the deterioration of the organism. The waking state is returned, the mind remains heavy and oppressed, and the body is unrefreshed. Those who suffer the gut when they sleep complain upon waking of being hag-ridden and wearied. It is as if they had been spurred, or whipped, they say, lashed and beaten all through the night. They rise with foul mouths and white tongues, with belchings and yawnings. They spit and heave and look about or cradle themselves and hardly move at all. Their spirit for life is gone and the curative of sleep is denied. This was another reason why I fed him paste. The alimentary organs must be unburdened if the mind is to be unburdened. The gut and its attendants should be at ease, quiet, and ideally clean through. I have prescriptions for this too. Certainly, the guts must not be filled with wind, nor choler, otherwise known as yellow bile, nor superfluous chyle, or the sleep will be peevish and the outlook irascible upon waking. Unconcocted chyle circulates its milk, a fatty substance, first to the bowels, then to its vessels, and delivers convulsions, not always with sensible pain, as well as nightmares, flatus, and oppressions of the spirit. For most patients, the cause of all difficulty is their diet, and not their mind. Even those scholars I have treated suffer more often than not as a result of their diet rather than as a consequence of their mind's activities, although most scholars would like to think that if they suffer, it must be the suffering of excess thought, of their great mental exertions, which afflicts them. The state of thinking is indeed a state of killing, and scholars do suffer from it. But scholars are also habitual grazers and suffer more from the gut. They are often the worst to treat because they will not accept that almost all human suffering has an alimentary origin, and that if the mind thinks, it largely thinks for alimentary reasons. Most thoughts are sublimated alimentary impulses. The animal ingests what it will and expels what it suffers, it is a simple enough tenet, but scholars will not learn it. Scholars would have themselves believe that they feast primarily on philosophic materials, and if they suffer gas, it is the vapours of the mind and not the vapours of the gut that pass out of them with such force. They are only half right. The effects of the diet on the gut may be delayed, and this makes the workings of the gut and its afflictions harder to pinpoint with certainty. What is eaten the day before, or even some days before that, may linger in the system long after the eating of it is forgotten. The animal functions of the human body do not submit easily to inspection, and yet, it is a simple enough fact of the life and growth of organisms, as well as their diminishment and eventual decay, that they cannot exist without bringing their exterior into relation with their interior. The exterior economy of forces must be brought into the economy of the insides. And so too in reverse. This is why the mouth has such import. It is why we dwell upon the mouth. The mouth is the point of access and one of the chief organs of expulsion. What is outside will penetrate by way of the mouth and be either expelled by the gut or incorporated into the fibres and the ligatures. Each body is, after all, nothing but gathered up materials. How else would offspring enlarge themselves into adults if they did not gather materials and incorporate them. The body is the co-opted exterior, and it brings within itself, by co-option, the corruption of what it absorbs. Minerals must be corrupted by dissolution just as the fibres of flesh and plant must be corrupted by their own dissolution. The body of the organism is dependent on the dissolution of its environment and can only be treated on that basis. There are some very obvious, very simple, consequences of this realisation. The paste I administered was given on this principle indeed. I submitted the foods I had him consume to advance corruption so to lessen the work of his weakened system in absorbing them. But the mind operates on very similar principles too. It can only absorb what it corrupts. As the mind incorporates what it perceives, it can only do so on the basis of a prior dissolution. Think of the mind as a vessel that takes in its exterior. It must surely liquify what it incorporates, boil it down, and then extrude only the finest scum of that concoction, otherwise the vessel would fill with a few short glances at the world it sees. Room must be made as well—if we think of the mind as a vessel—to allow the incorporation of forces. We may think of speech as a mechanism of removal, of the mouth as the first orifice of expulsion, and of the necessity of talking as the necessity of making room in the mind for its growth within the confines of the head. The skull cavity is the ultimate limit that halts growth and maintains humanity in its comparative ignorance. Trepanning—the boring of a hole into the head—has to be the most audacious of refusals of the limits of the mind. False testimony ascribes the origins of trepanning to the expelling of spirits, the treatment of madness, or to the evacuation of inner pressure. The origins of trepanning are poorly understood indeed. Few realise how the boring of skulls originated as a practice to rival the great philosophic inquisitors—the pioneers of philosophic thought before its systematisation—who themselves sought to take thought and perception to its extremities but had or only employed to that purpose their means of intellection for tools, a reflective pose that will never discover anything of the nature of existence from the serene aspect. Trepanation produced the first true philosophers of experience. The expulsion of spirits and the alleviation of madness were, if they were stated as reasons, mere stand-ins for a more serious purpose, a purpose which could not be articulated to the satisfaction of their non-trepanning peers. Perhaps too few survived even as the construction of the trephine, the circular auger, was perfected. But as they sat and had themselves bored out, they perceived levels of stimulus that the mind will not usually admit and saw the energies of the vastness outside of them with unfiltered clarity. The usual condition of disorder, the specific human condition which I treat, is nonetheless, and more typically, that of the alimentary outlook, so said. I remind myself of this in order to recall myself. When I visit patients, I encounter them first as alimentary beings, and only second as thinking creatures. All manifestations of the thinking being must be investigated, first of all, for their alimentary causes. And so, to inspect this patient not as an alimentary patient, but as another kind of sufferer, was indeed heresy of a kind, at least within the orbit of my professional understanding. It was a radical departure from my usual practice to look at the patient before me not as an alimentary patient, but as a patient whose suffering had non-material origins. His disease, I came to think, would be more profitably treated as a non-material disease, or what is known outside my profession as a spiritual affliction. This places me at the borders of my craft, although it may turn out that spiritual afflictions are of the order of vapours, and so have a worldly basis too. The advancement of medicine is at crucial points in its history a heretic operation, and this may well be one of those historic junctures.

Knowing that my patient was not yet strong enough to tell me of the midden I asked for more details concerning the conditions of the weed. The conditions of the weed were described in the report, he said. The report, he repeated after I shook him again. So tell me what it said, I replied. He complained abstractly of the sound I made, but I insisted, doing so not by asking, it was a mistake to say, so tell me what it said. By telling him to tell me what it said I caused him to complain about the sound I made. He complained abstractly at my words, mere noises to his ears. I asked him about the weed, and he moaned again at the noise. I could only encourage him to speak by repeating what he said. To hear more about the weed I had to repeat what he had already said about the weed for encouragement. This was how I brought him to speak in the first place. But I would forget myself and ask him again questions that were mere frustrations, but once I remembered myself, I returned to repetitions and imitations. I wet his lips as I went on demanding details concerning the weed by this method. Many of the words he came to say were the words dictated by his employer, or so he said. These are the words of my employer, he would tell me. This is what my employer said on this or that topic. Soon he was fully awake again and taken by his recollection to a fuller account of the weed.

The weed, my employer dictated, he said, does not submit to rigid description. It is a saline substance. This is the most definite thing that may be said about it, but that is not saying much since saline substances are known to be unstable in their form, migrating from one place to another by processes of dispersal and subsequent coalescence. Consequently, the borders of saline substances can be hard to determine—they shift. This itself is hardly a definite description of the nature of saline substances, as must be the case, indeed, since nature herself might be characterised in a similar way, she proceeds by minute gradations. As soon as nature is described in a manner approaching her complexity, the border between one thing and another disappears. Decisive marks, or definite borders in nature are rare, and where they are noted, they occur as gross simplifications of these imperceptible differences.

The natural life of the islanders might be seen as an extension of their surroundings, my employer said. To the extent they produce objects that are recognisable as human artifices, he dictated, and to the extent theirs is a culture, it proceeds only by imperceptible differences and has no definite characteristics. The glass objects they create do indeed freeze the gradual flux of their cultural life, but across the surfaces of these objects their form is fluid as if those surfaces were still in motion. These creations are discarded almost as soon as they are crafted and have no enduring significance as objects to those who made them. The weed that went into them is first dried, either in the sun during the summer months, or in the lofts of the glasshouses during the winter. When sufficiently crisp by the heat of the sun, or the heat of the glassworks and their ovens, the weed is set on fire. The fire placement is confined to a hole in the ground, initially, until the weed is so mounded up within it, and then to grow out, so that it forms a pyre above ground. This pyre is loaded with subsequent weed as the inner parts combust and lower, these themselves first melted by the violence of the heat, then reduced to ash by the flames that penetrate the mass and extend to the outermost parts. The pyre is at last left to smoke, and its molten innards allowed to smoulder and then cool. It forms a solid mass that is hauled out so that the next fire might be lit if the burning fields are still to be used, which is by no means assured.

We have seen pyres abandoned for no apparent reason, even though the digging of the pits takes considerable effort, and even though it makes no sense in terms of the expenditure of resources to move on to new burning fields and dig fresh pits. It might be that the islanders become distracted by the next stage, which involves the reduction of the solid mass to a fine powder. The lump from the fire pit is taken away by those who work at the glassworks, or it is taken by those who burn the weed themselves to the pounding ground, usually a bare rock. Larger lumps tend to attract greater numbers, and cause more distraction, and might be associated with the abandonment of the pits and the burning fields. Smaller, but oddly-shapen lumps may have a similar effect, with large crowds of islanders following needlessly at first, since merely two or three islanders are required for the carrying, and perhaps four or five for the pounding, during which they take turns.

The tools used for the pounding vary from tree stumps or nearby rocks to lumps of iron or bricks that have been taken from an abandoned glasshouse. There is considerable ash ingestion during the pounding as the clouds it makes lift up around the islanders cavorting within the mist. Dust is raised and coats the face, transforming each into a crust. As the pounding continues, former grimaces and cries are cracked and reshaped by the arrival of fresh dust and lines of sweat. These faces might profitably be inspected if only they would be still, each mask a lived description, and a short, encrusted history of the emotions of the frolic.

Those overcome by ash inhalation and dust eating fall away from the centre of the pounding and are replaced by others who continue the pounding and eat the pall in turn. When the crowds are large enough those struck by ash inhalation form a ring around the pounding. They become a circumference of exhausted islanders, gasping against the ash in their lungs and heaving against the accumulated ash in their stomachs. During the pounding the lump is gradually reduced to smaller pieces that are placed back on the rock and reduced in turn. Meanwhile, the powder grows in heaps about the pounding place. The encircling islanders, subdued by the ash eating and the ash effects, gather on all fours and belch and vomit the dust back out from inside them. This half-digested ash falls out as a lump with the digestive juices following from their ash-encrusted lips. Each face now hardened off, the skin toughened and grown outward by its layering and the wetting and drying of sweat, then turns to consider its companion not long finished belching and vomiting ash itself. The islanders set back down and orient their faces to talk. They seat themselves around the pounding which continues at the centre, and as they sit, they begin to speak. With their facial features fixed, their speech is focused and directed, and may very well be described as communicative, not the wandering speech of their walking. The islanders sit and talk and exchange words that carry messages and incur responses, stopping only at intervals to belch another ash pellet, returning from all fours to a seating position and the resumption of talk. Many great words are spoken. Cicero has been heard here intoned, and some Baconian science has been spoken.

An extraordinary description, I said, to which he looked back blankly. It is what my employer dictated, he replied.

HIS VISIT TO THE GLASSHOUSES.

My hosts were beginning to lose their patience. The initial excitement of finding him and then of treating him with vomits and purges, calling the doctor from inland and seeing the doctor come at such personal cost, had clearly diminished as my stay lengthened. It might be added that my pay, which was my due, never materialised. When I first arrived, it was clear they were impressed by my presence. I could see that when I descended from the coach with my doctor's bag they were roused by the sight of the doctor and his luggage, and that they were equally taken, if not more so, by the fact it was the four of them and none other who had called for me and my bag by sending a mule across the moors. They had not seen a man descend a coach quite like I had done before, not for some time at least. A coach arrival from inland was an unusual event for these people, cut off from the rest of our large island nation by the moors and the hills and the neglect of our governors.

They lived secluded in their fishing hamlet, trading fish with the neighbouring settlement on hand-drawn carts with solid block wheels. Even the spokes of the wheels of my coach moved them to comment. These spokes surely struck them as elegant, although they were rudimentary wheels for sure. The horse too. It was a pitiful beast, abused, a case in animal ruin, but it stood over them and struck them with awe at its comparative strength and size. As the coach made its way towards them, my hosts stood before the rest of the inhabitants, before the wreck of the coble, before their house where the patient lay upstairs. They were surrounded by their neighbours and fellows and all looked on as the coach rocked and pitched about over the track that led down to the building by the jetty and the launch. This coach I arrived with was a mere glorified cart, it was the best I could hire for the journey and would be an embarrassment in other circumstances, but to them clearly a vehicle of distinction. They looked at the coach and marvelled. Its axles creaked and ached and spoke to me of the pain of travel. But they heard the same axles sing of their distances and better roads than these rough tracks—paved roads, grand façades, and lavish squares. And then after it came to a halt, as the beast came to stand, exhale, and continued to sweat, I myself descended, and the very manner in which I did so, even against the fact of the doctor's bag, only roused them further. The doctor's bag was nothing alongside how I moved as I emerged and alighted. I might have left my doctor's bag in the coach and there would have been very nearly the same effect upon them. How I exited that coach clearly struck them as distinctive. Against the sight of the coach, and against the sight of the doctor's bag which secured my professional status, my descent was easily an event of still greater importance. My feet were only on the steps of the coach, and they marvelled already. I placed my feet—the steps were small, the coach was parked at a slant—and the care with which I placed them obviously struck my onlookers as significant. Simply my shoes impressed them. The buckles struck them as distinguished, as yet another announcement of my importance. These are the shoes of my visiting rounds, and not my town shoes which are more refined. They are the pair I wear when I expect to encounter muck such as their hamlet dirt, but still these shoes were far better than those who received me would usually see upon other persons and their own feet most definitely. I looked at their feet and the poor manner in which they were shod. These feet caked with the usual rural filth. Their feet moved backwards as I descended. I saw them move back a little to receive me. I felt how I was received as I made down those steps. My hosts were quite obviously taken with themselves as the doctor made his way towards them. I was consumed by the events of my journey but still could see the impression I gave and knew it was a good one. I left the coach severely annoyed by the driver and in a state of high agitation, that is to say, in a condition that inland would strike any onlooker as harassed, and ungainly, and inconsolable. I had been greatly worn by the coachman's incessant questioning, addressed from his box seat, the reigns limp in his hands as he asked me, my doctor, what I thought of this fatal accident, or that fatal accident, gesturing this way and that, because along our route he could easily spot the potential for each fatal accident which must greet us at a moment's inattention, the casualties of which he could remember too, having seen his worst fears realised in most fatal spots of the moors over the years at this bend or that where he had come across upturned carriages, crumpled horses, and human fatalities. This drop is surely a fatal accident, that bend is too, and that bank beyond it, and the cliff we just passed, and so on. But would this fatal accident be a sudden death or a lingering death, he would say to me. In your medical opinion, my coachman went on, would we be met with a lingering death at this bend, that cliff, this precipice, that river, or a sudden death, and which would I prefer if I had the choice. In your medical opinion would you prefer a lingering death or a sudden one, he asked me. Which would you recommend. Based on your medical training and your knowledge of such things as these, is a lingering death or a sudden death preferable. Having surely in your career attended the former and seen the results of the latter, which would you stake your claim on. Should I hope to linger on or expire straightaway, he said and as he said this he again turned about on his box seat, staring at me, as we hurtled on. He stared at me, asking me this, as the beast itself chose our route. Because I have never quite managed to side one way or the other. If we were to pass this way after dark, he said, a fatal accident would be assured, he told me, because I would not see the perils of our route. Even in the light of day this track will easily turn us over. But I could not predict, said he, if it would be lingering or sudden, nor can I be sure which I should want. As he said that again, he turned back to his horse, stating once more that he could never quite make up his mind, and because he could not make it up, he would rather not travel after dark whereupon the choice would be made for us by the darkness and would occur before he had the opportunity to properly think it through. After the tortures of this journey and as I left his cart, my care at the steps of the coach was only the care of a man who did not wish to fall down those steps with exhaustion and irritation. But to my hosts, again, it was a sign of distinction how I lowered myself down to the dirt of their fishing hamlet. I walked towards the group—the entirety of the hamlet—and my hosts gestured to the door. I suspect they almost bowed in response to my own movement, flinching into action as I ducked my head to get through the low doorway and into the building they occupied. My hosts ushered me up the staircase with apparent pleasure and presented their patient with pride, or rude affectation, describing what they had done for him, how they had purged and vomited him—they did this on the threshold, they said, and they did it only after they had unclothed him and carried him through the hamlet, they did it before their neighbours too, so they let me know, those who had offered to help with the carrying, but the four were too proud at that point to accept, so I gathered, and the onlookers had to content themselves with watching the carrying, the purging, and the vomiting, but not participating in it. They carried him laid upon the largest piece of the wrecked coble he was found with. It was because there were four of them that they managed it. They tied ropes to the wrecked coble, they said, and dragged those ropes over their shoulders, but when the wreck began to rock, they raised it up, and carried it directly. With the timber itself resting from one shoulder to the next, like a coffin, they added, it no longer rocked and was entirely still. They walked the wreck with my patient attached and did so with not the slightest wobble at all, I was assured.

On the first morning after I sat with the patient, my hosts brought up a peeled egg on a dish together with a small pot of salt. All four entered to look at me and look at the patient and see how the doctor received his egg. It was an appallingly meagre breakfast, I had been up all night, but I accepted it with good grace and my acceptance and grace seemed to impress them once more. They had arrived with the egg and I received it graciously. The egg was presented by my hosts and I thanked them for it. I did not wait for my next meal—if there would be such a thing—but went to the inn or what functioned as the inn where the food was equally rudimentary but there was more of it. I was served a potato, with salt, preceded by a broth. The landlady asked if I would like an egg with it and I accepted my second egg of the day. I sat with the egg, the potato, and the salt, and she told me about the fire. She first mentioned it when she delivered the broth. I must tell you about the fire, she said. Do not let me forget to tell you about the fire. You will have seen the ruin on your way to the inn, and surely now you will wish to find out how it happened. And then she mentioned it all over when she delivered the potato. I must tell you of the fire, she said again. And after that she fetched the egg. I must tell you about the fire, she told me once more as if I still needed telling. And then, at last, she did. It was in this way that her account of the fire came with the egg although I had been thinking about it since the broth. She stood peeling it as I sat with the potato, telling me of the destruction the fire brought. It was a terrible fire, she said, as I sat looking at the potato, waiting for the egg to be peeled. As I pinched a little skin from the surface of the potato but then decided it too hot yet for proper eating and so resumed my looking at the thing, the landlady stood over me telling me ever more of her tale. On the second morning, back at the room with the patient, pretty much the same happened. The egg arrived already peeled by my hosts with the salt in a pot by the side. I thanked them for it. My four hosts nodded, satisfied again by my gracious acceptance of their meagre breakfast and backed out of the room they had given use of, doing so with a glance at the patient and another at my doctor's bag. The bag was open to reveal the apparatus I carried which caught their eye as they left. On the third morning the bag still impressed them and was again open for their inspection. On the fourth I inadvertently closed the bag, and they left in a state of obvious disgruntlement. I was given the distinct impression my hosts were less impressed by my being there, so on the fifth I made sure my doctor's bag was open wide. I arranged the highly sophisticated medical apparatus I carried so that it poked out the top a bit. This did catch their attention as my four hosts filed in and then filed out, leaving me with the peeled egg and the small pot for the sprinkling of salt, as usual. On the sixth they actually came over and peered in the bag and nodded at it. On the seventh, suspecting this would not suffice to impress them a further time, I laid out my instruments at the foot of the bed, paying particular attention to the more violent or demonstrably intricate apparatus I carried. After seeing this outlay, they left more deferential in manner than on the sixth and fifth morning, or the fourth, and even the third, but still not approaching the deference of the first morning and the second. In subsequent days their behaviour remained largely in line with the lower deference levels of the fourth morning, that is, they showed me some disgruntlement but still brought the egg. The four of them filed in to look at me and the patient and left me with the egg and the salt. I went to the inn or what functioned as the inn in subsequent days too, as was now my custom, and ate the broth and the potato and my second egg of each day. The landlady stood by me, peeling the egg, telling me again of the dreadful fire, a fire I had again been reminded about at least since the broth, but would not hear any details of that day until the egg. Eventually, upon looking at the egg that the landlady gave me, I grew suspicious of the egg I received that morning earlier. Either one was growing in size, or the other was diminishing. The egg which I ate for my subsequent meal of the day at the inn was decidedly bigger, or so I thought, when compared to the egg I was presented with in the morning. I did not have the two before me for direct comparison, but as I sat in the inn, and the landlady stood by me telling me about the fire, and then retreating to her position behind the counter, I could be sure that this egg, her egg, was bigger than the egg my hosts had given me that morning. The landlady stood over me, as usual, peeling the egg with her fingers, and as she stood beside me, that is to say, even before the egg landed on my plate, I was sure it was a bigger egg than the one they gave me earlier in the room with the patient. This struck me acutely, because on the first day when I arrived at the inn and sat, and as the landlady came over with the egg and peeled it with her fingers, I remember thinking how similar that egg was in size to the egg they gave me first thing. I remember thinking to myself how small the chances were that the egg would be exactly the same as the one I received in the morning. I thought just how much more likely it would be that the eggs differed in size, given how much eggs vary in proportion according to the condition of the hen that lays it, the variations of its diet and so on. Within a single sequence issuing from the same hen, eggs must surely vary. Eggs from the same hen will vary according to the variable effort that has been expended on the egg laid just before and the egg to be laid after which may exert a pressure on the egg between. I have no experience of hens, but I suspect that the same hen lays different sized eggs due to these intervening pressures. Different hens will also lay different sized eggs and there was more than one egg laying hen in this hamlet. That was undoubtable. On the second day when I accepted the addition of an egg to my meal, I remember thinking how remarkably similar this egg was again to the egg that my hosts had delivered that morning. How could the same sized egg be delivered in the inn, for my second meal, I thought. It was surely improbable.

The egg on the second day was delivered with the broth. Occasionally it would happen this way, with the egg thereby preceding the potato. She started telling me about the fire when I had the broth, as she peeled the egg, talking about the dreadful fire. There came, she said, a sudden and dreadful fire. There happened a sudden and dreadful fire to break out in the dwelling house across the street. The thatch was smoking and then the building was consumed. The flames came out of the windows and the doors and then it was all eaten up, she said, peeling the egg. You must have seen the wreckage now. There is nothing left of the dwelling house, just the blackened roof timbers and the fireplace and the chimney.

The wind was high that day, she told me. As I remember, the wind was up. This made it worse. Within the space of an hour it burnt down and consumed the house, she went on, working the egg as she talked. The wind took in at the windows and fed the fire. It consumed the house and all it contained. The furniture, the cots, the table, the chairs. All of it gone. The best wearing apparel was gone too. The fire consumed the whole house with the linen and all the other household goods. There was linen on the line too when the fire took. That burnt as well. So too did the leaves of the tree in the yard. Every single one, incinerated, and then the rest of it. Even the outer walls of her own inn were hot to touch, she said. It was just over the street after all, the landlady told me. You might have boiled an egg in the afterglow. The egg she delivered was now floating in the broth, sliced in two. It was surely the same sized egg, I thought. This must be the same egg, I decided, as the landlady talked on and told me about the copperware that melted and became misshapen. The pots were still on their hooks, or some of them were, but each was warped and beyond use. As I ate the broth and she walked back to the counter after telling me this, her account strayed not at all that much from that delivered on the first day and would be little different from the one she would again repeat on the third, and the fourth, and so on. But I continued to think as I ate her broth about that remarkable fact of the egg. This was the same egg, effectively the same egg, as the one that morning. Even as I sat there with the landlady standing beside me, breathing over me as she peeled the egg with her fingers all the while telling of the fire, I began to suspect that the egg she peeled was of a very similar size, if not identical to the egg delivered that morning by my hosts. On this second day my hosts were still extremely deferential and I ate that meagre meal to their pleasure. On the third and fourth day I did not think all that much about it, and by the fifth I had stopped comparing. It was only as the eggs no longer matched up in my memory and my perception of their size, that I began to notice the size of them once more. I became certain of the fact that the landlady was either bringing me larger eggs each day, and so showing me favour as she stood there, standing improbably close to my shoulder as she prepared the day's egg, or my hosts were delivering a smaller egg each day, which made the landlady's egg look bigger. Eventually I decided that my hosts were most certainly bringing me smaller eggs, which did not rule out the landlady bringing me ones that were slightly bigger. Their adjustment in the quantity of salt decided it for me. I was sure that the little salt pot came with a smaller portion now, and eventually the salt came without the pot, just heaped instead. It was at last merely sprinkled on the dish with the egg, with there not being enough salt now for any kind of heaping. After that, the egg arrived unpeeled by my hosts, and I knew by that point I had overstayed my welcome. The four no longer felt anything for the patient and, presumably too, no longer drew any further awe or respect from their neighbours as their having been the ones who had raised the man and carried him off the beach, and who had done the purging and vomiting, and lastly, as the hamlet folk who had distinguished themselves as my employers, or then as my hosts, and increasingly as my begrudging cohabitants, since they had failed to pay me, were becoming worse at hosting me, and I had yet no means of leaving the hamlet. The wreck of the coble leant against the wall outside their house was gone.

Lifting the egg, I heard the door close and listened to their footsteps retreat, all four sets, as they made their usual descent for the lower part of the house. The egg is unpeeled, I said, holding it higher for the patient to see. We are no longer welcome, I told my patient, who looked back, barely with the strength to raise an arm, or sit, now his condition was worsened. This egg declares by the fact of it that we are no longer welcome, I said again to be sure he understood. His eyes followed the egg as I talked moving it back and forth for him to see. I inspected the egg from one side and the other. As I moved the unpeeled egg about his vision, I caused the whites of his eyes to slide out from one side and the other. He could hardly move his head—it was set in place with his returned fatigue. This egg was peeled yesterday, I said to him, moving the egg. Yesterday they still peeled the egg, I told him. Today they did not. We must take care now and keep good watch of our hosts.

On this point and all others relating to our immediate context, he was entirely silent. I could elicit nothing from him about his own reckoning of the egg, its significance, of the changing attitude of our hosts, their neglect of the egg, or the lack of salt. He would say nothing of that. His eyes followed the egg but he would not comment just as he had not commented on anything about himself, or about me, or about his stay here. The only responses I received were to prompts concerning the island. If I told him to raise his arm, he would not raise his arm. When I told him to move his head, he would not move it. His head only ever moved, like his arm, from the effects of his telling which made the tendons stretch and the jugulars fill with blood. To feed him paste I massaged his jaw to cause his mouth to open. It did not open to receive the paste as he saw the paste arrive or because I told him to open his mouth. There was no opening of his mouth by these more usual means. I could not prompt him to open it other than causing the jaw to move by manipulating its joint. His eyes followed me, but they did not transmit instruction, just as his ears did not carry my commands. Only by speaking of the island as he had told it to me, and with some of the very words he had used, could I communicate with him, or prompt him, and cause his mouth to open and then to speak. I caused him to speak just as I massaged his jaw to administer the paste.

It was in this way I learnt more of the glasshouses by speaking the word glasshouse to him. It was still easy to forget and revert to more customary practice. I could not say, tell me of the glasshouses. That had no effect, of course. But I said it. I had forgotten myself again. I had to make my requests differently. Of the glasshouse, the glasshouses, in the glasshouse, I said, massaging his ears with the sound of it. This speaking of the glasshouses is what made his condition worsen as I insisted on it, saying, about the glasshouses, these glasshouses, on glasshouses, when the glasshouse, and so on, to enliven his speech when it became exhausted.

His stick, my patient told me, or so I gathered, is what drove me to the glasshouse. That stick hounded me about the island as I heard its tapping. For days I was free of the sound of it and then it would arrive, first at a distance, then halting, and then resuming a little closer, and finally close enough to make me flee. The tapping of his stick was seeking me out. My employer was criss-crossing the island looking for me, the accomplice who had taken down the report that he left for the islanders to find, knowing as he did so how it would change them and make them unpredictable towards us. I skirted the main house of the island but did not enter it. I avoided the islanders as they moved about and gradually migrated from one region of industry to another fresh site of work. I skirted the burning fields and avoided the water's edges where the weed was gathered. I tracked across others where it was not. One time my employer approached on the shore, picking across the rocks, bent over to be sure of his footing. I was still unseen but had a long retreat to make, so I relented from my weed avoidance and gathered up the dried weed from the highest water mark and covered myself with it and the flies that crawl and lick the crispen mass. My employer passed me with his stick, and I waited, enduring their little inspections, and then, finally, lifted myself up and picked the creatures off me.

I heard the stick again, days later. I was now far inland and roving close to the islanders. This time I fled to their security, knowing he avoided them too, or at least had no interest any more in studying them close by. The islanders did not appear to see me as I ran into their glasshouse, even as I fell over the blowing rods they used and crept around the furnace to the inner wall, furthest from the entrance. The islander with the billows set to work, standing in the trench that leads to the furnace door, a clay tile. It was open to admit the air that the islander pushed in from the spout. Another raised the lid of the furnace from a hook and poured in the sea-coal which seemed to vaporise outright. The furnace was dug into the floor but rose above their heads, the fire inside built to the levels of heat that melt sand. The walls of the furnace creaked and then the floor around began to groan with its expansion. With the lid up, and the glory hole open, the room was well glared at, enough to shadow the islanders on the walls. When the lid was down, and the tile placed back into the hole, the room was dark against the light of the doorway. This darkness made the heat seem improbable as it burnt my face as the sun will burn and dried and seared my eyes. I shrank from the heat and held my arm over my face to protect myself from it. As I held my arm like that, I heard a tap at the threshold, unmistakably his stick, and I looked to see my employer standing in the light, misshapen by the heat between us. The billows went and I lowered my eyes. A rod was entered through the glory hole to grab a glob. I heard them take it out and blow and rotate the molten mass back and forth, shaping it, turning it over, and placing it back in. As we had written, this mass of molten glass is taken from the edges of the crucible, not the centre as is otherwise usual, but where the lesser glass languishes. Here it collects together the impurities that glassworkers would usually avoid. Another islander crushes glass remainders from earlier works in a shallow pit by sitting at its edge, dropping them in, and letting the heel fall to break them. The molten glob, now part inflated by the blowing, is rolled into these pieces, and the entire ensemble placed back into the furnace where the mass amalgamates, forming a fresh orb with newly characterised surfaces that integrate the memories and trace effects of the destroyed remainders. The glass objects almost always incorporate an element of the remainders, and not just the newly made glass from the sand and the ash. The destruction of legacies of glass production—past work and creation which were themselves based on the destruction of past work and creation before them—is the condition under which anything new, never truly new, is blown. Every orb contains the artefacts of previous glassworks laid and melted across its surface. This is how the past is burnt into the present. It is a unique and specific encounter of liquids that solidify together, bearing the circumstance over which they are cooled. I looked again and saw he was gone from the doorway. The islanders had surely seen him as they surely saw me. They saw us both as the glob was taken. The blow iron which held the cooling glass was rested on a block before another islander for cracking off, and then to carry to the annealing lehr where the object would be left to heal. The islanders passed each annealed thing between them and examined their creation with gestures and glances, the same faces that not long before were cracked with dust and run with sweat at the pounding of the ash. The glass orbs tended to already crizzle as they were handled, the surface roughened by the islanders' palms. This would begin to cloud any transparency it had with networks of scratches that gradually obscured the vision of the insides. And then one islander stood, held out the piece, and dropped it. Some broke immediately. Others survived to be gathered later and crushed when the islanders walked across the island in lines, prodding the grass with their blow irons, gathering all the objects they could find not for recasting but for throwing in the midden.

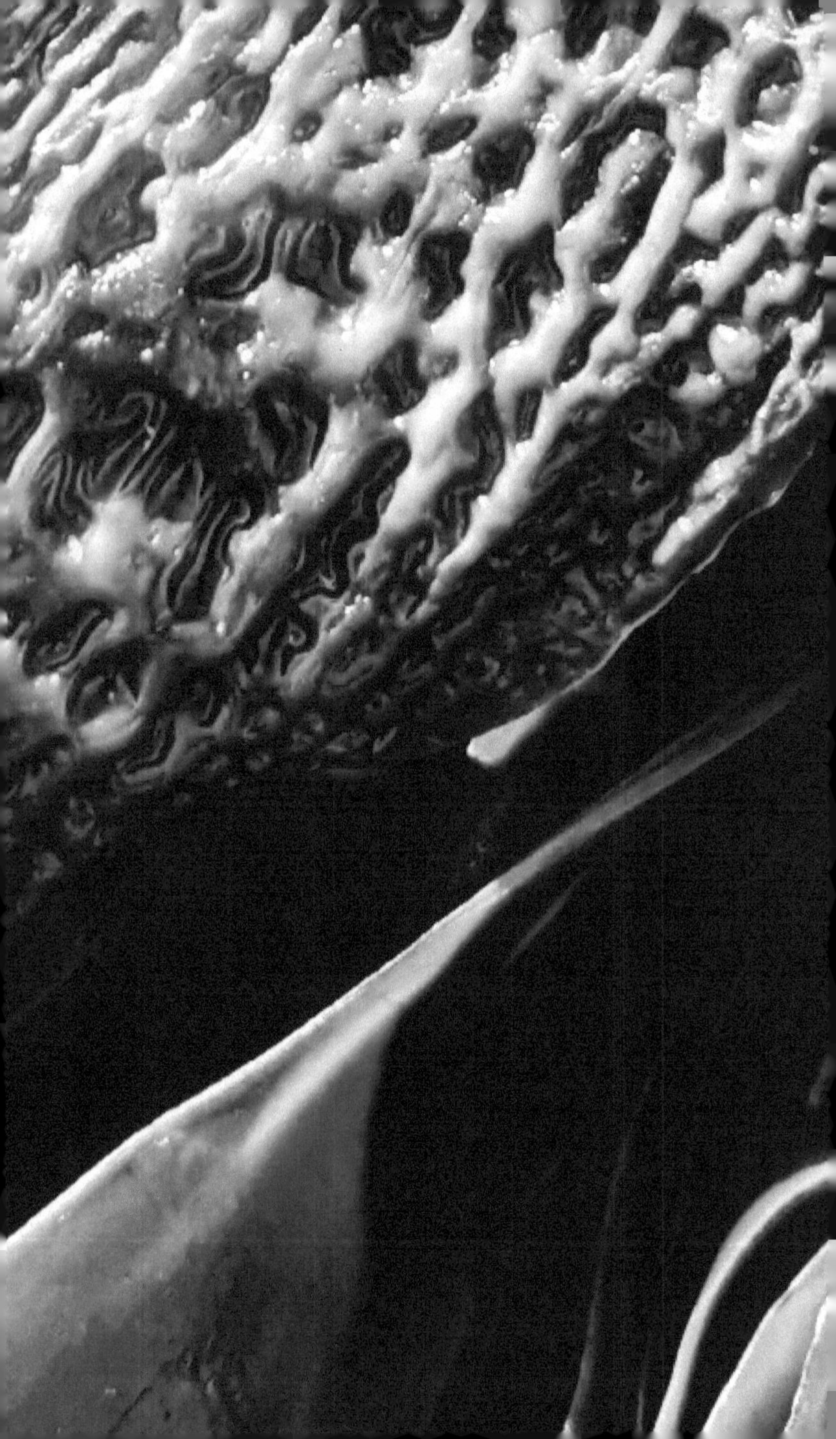

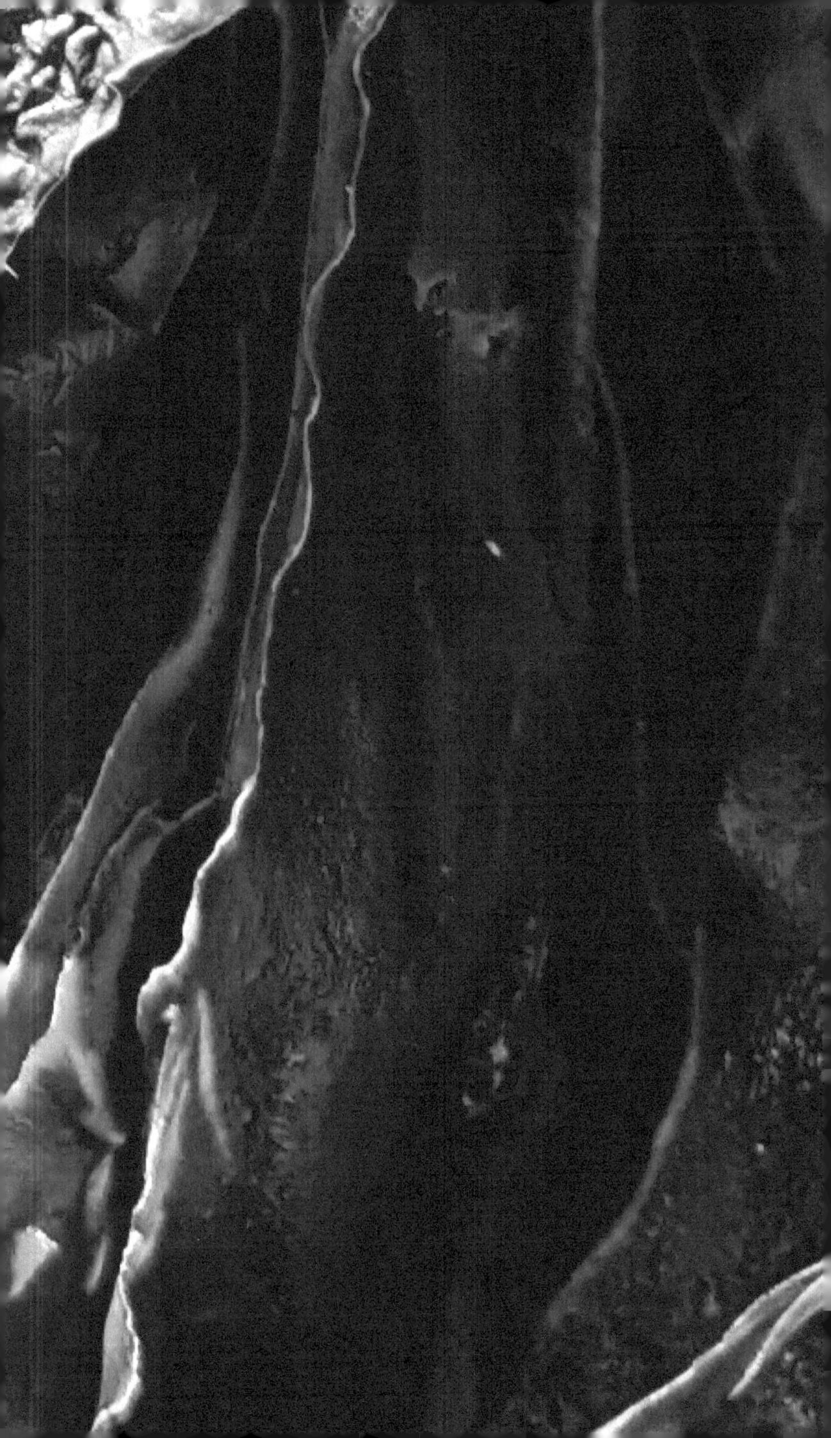

Oɴ ʟᴇᴀᴠɪɴɢ ᴛʜᴇ ᴍɪᴅᴅᴇɴ.

The midden, he told me, is under the island. I gathered from his description that this midden, or dumping ground, is spread across a vast chamber and reaches into a network of channels and rifts, some of which are dry, others wet at the base. This midden has been formed and has risen to extraordinary height directly below a crack in the surface where past and present islanders have disposed of their waste. Through that fault line the waste has fallen into the chamber, producing a cone-shaped pile of detritus, a depositional mound resembling a hill. Down its slope each fresh in-fall fell and slipped until it came to a stop. This was how the cone grew both in its height but also in width until it reached the edges of the chamber and then crept outwards into the smaller caverns and passages at its perimeters.

When I was first lowered through the crack, the extent of the midden hill was still unknown to us. We did not know that the islanders went there to throw things in. We had not yet seen them do it. My employer had me go down, and I hung there, just under the rift, looking from the ceiling of the chamber to the black below. Only the midden top was visible from the black, the rest of it receding quickly out of the light. The peak appeared to be made of glass. As became clearer, it was made of those crizzled remainders we had seen the islanders produce in their glassworks. They were largely its surface where I saw it, with only occasional interruptions by other debris. These remainders reflected in their multitudes the light of the crack and in their many thousands the yellow flame of the small lantern I held. However, as I came down upon its surface, the glass remainders fell away from my landing place and caused a small slide of disturbed waste. I could see beneath it a surface of shell, which meant the glass midden was a mere crust laid over a more ancient shell mound. It was mainly shell fragments from there on down, with occasional bone, discarded pottery, and other artefacts.

Later my employer told me of his conclusions. He called them down the fissure. This was once a mountain, not an island, my employer shouted down. From what you have retrieved it must be so. There was that femur, he said, it came from a land animal not now living on this island and likely never living here given how it was a creature that lived upon great plains nothing like what we have here about us. Do you recall the femur, he said. Well now I have examined it and this femur indicates the future of our dig. The sea around was receded and the higher land looked across vast plains. In our excavations there will come a point, he said, where the shell midden will entirely stop and become animal remains, or if shell persists, these fragments will be from distant seas and not the immediate shoreline which will have gone, will no longer exist in this ancient time our dig is revealing. These carcases you will come across, and which the femur anticipates, will have been hauled from the reaches before those reaches were flooded by the sea. They will have been taken from the plains of what later became the sea floor to this single mount, to this crack in the earth, our hole in this basalt rock which received everything they threw down it and never was made full because of its size. From what you have excavated so far, my employer told me, it is clear the present islanders are only the most recent to throw in at the midden. This crack in the crust of the planet has been in use so long as humans have walked the land, as every bucket you fill and return to me does show and as the mere size of this thing must surely indicate. There is no midden to match this hill. No midden besides this one could boast continuous use across such an extended period of time. I had dug a metre that my employer said was equivalent to the age of the oldest oak that still stands and lives. By the size of the midden itself, taking the cone to its fullest proportions, many hundreds if not thousands of oaks had grown and fallen and seeded subsequent oaks that grew to their greatest age and fell and rotted in turn. The size of the midden declares it, my employer said.

I made the descent through the crack but could not return by the same route unaided. We first tied the rope to a rock above ground at the side of the fissure. My employer knotted it and I looked on, consenting to the knot and its purchase. He was sure there was something down there, my employer told me. He said he could sense its vastness by the quality of the air that came up. There is something down there, he said, as he dropped the rope down the crack. He did not call it a midden yet, he could not have anticipated a midden, or not a midden hill. Go on, have a look, he said, gesturing to the rope. He handed me the lantern which I clipped to my belt. Take the rope, and have a look, he repeated, so I turned with my back to the cleft in the rock and took the rope in my hands, edging backwards to the brink, my employer standing by the rock where the rope was anchored, nodding me on. As I lowered myself over the gap and walked my feet down it, the rope creaked and rubbed at the sides of the rift. My grip slipped downwards from each knot and the run of rope to the next.

I was in the shadowed part of the cut, now stationary, hanging. The rope pulled the palms of my hands around their edges. The edges of the cut, its walls, were creviced and fractured with miniature rifts that let inward horizontally and were filled at their bases with dirt. The light from above did not penetrate these side recesses nor did the light of my lantern that was hanging below me shine there as my feet walked the edges. I then looked below and saw the top. All that emerged from the black was the crest of it. There is the top of something, I shouted up. It looks like a mound of glass. Go on, he replied, descend further. The crack falls away to the top of something, I told him, but there is a large gap between. From the base of the fissure to the top of whatever it is, there is a large gap. Find out what it is, my employer said. My hands grabbed and slid from one knot to the next again when finally my foothold slipped into the void. And so it was I fell bodily against the sides of the walls of the cut.

The sides, I shouted, I'm hanging, pull me up. I can't pull you up, he shouted back, go on. There was no air left in my lungs to shout with, hanging, thoughtless— the crucified cannot hardly think, that was evident now—my palms still pulled around their edges and drawn to the fingers, descending into the black, the lantern not reaching the edges any more with its light. These walls had receded out of reflection as the fissure gave way to the chamber and here became ceiling. The roof of the cavern was hardly lit itself because the lantern, at my belt, did not cast upward, only outward, and to an extent downward. I could not look down any more in any case, my neck held in place by my raised shoulders, hanging, my grip failing, sliding to the next knot and over and to the next. Failing in my grasp from knot to rope to knot was how I reached the midden which yielded as I fell into it, still holding the rope but not hanging from it now, clutching it instead against the side of my head, from which it reached into and pulled at my lungs.

Then the rope was taken in. I hauled it back. Stop pulling, he said, I cannot haul you out. The rope returned with the bucket and the demand to fill it and before filling it to describe what I saw, which I did by shouts upward about the midden top, the glass remainders, and the shells beneath them. He asked me how big, and I told him the walls of the cavern were too far out to see. They remained unlit by the lantern and beyond its reach. He had me throw glass objects from the midden to hear where they hit, but there was no collision against the walls, instead there was sound, after an interval, of the glass hitting the slopes of the midden far down below the midden top, cumulating other materials in ballistic hops. This gave a good sense of the height of the midden, and its breadth, as the sound came from far below but also some distance across.

He kept me there, excavating, sleeping in the pit I dug, the crack above growing dark and then lit with the dawn, dark and then lit, my employer returning, lowering the bucket which contained food and a renewed demand to excavate. The spade I dug with fell and slid away down the midden sides, but he would not accept this loss of our equipment as a true description of my situation—he believed me pretending—and told me to dig still with the spade I knew to be lost but which he took as another plea for rescue. When you return, I shall dictate you what you have found, he shouted down. I will tell you, my employer told me, what you have returned me from your excavations. I will describe you your midden just as I lay it out here before me in successive piles.

Dark then lit, the rift in the ceiling, his voice, the rope, the bucket, the demand to dig. I dug with my hands in the pit that I slept in until the hole I had dug in the peak of the midden was impossible to climb out of. I told him that, I said I was now stranded in the hole I had dug in the peak of the hill. He told me back to dig at the sides so the hole would become a cut, a groove in the side of the mound. Dig then kick out the sides of your pit, he told me. Dig your pit into a groove, a cut, a trench. Once you have done that you will be able to climb out, he said. You can then leave your pit, your cut, by climbing up the banks of the midden. By his instruction I dug then pushed these side materials away down the banks of the midden hill, with the bucket now again returning materials only from the deepest points of the former pit which was now a cut, that is to say, from the innermost parts of that cut where the strata of waste materials tracked back evenly through time. I will tell you, my employer shouted from the rift. When you are returned to the surface, I will dictate what you have found down there. When you are on the surface again, my employer shouted to console my digging, I will dictate the midden to you. The fissure darkened again, I slept in the cut and my employer returned to our camp. He shouted at me to wake—the rift now lit, a crack of sky in the ceiling—and lowered the food, my breakfast. I will dictate, he shouted, as I pled with him to help me leave. You will return, he told me as I sat and ate the food, and I will dictate, he said. When you return, I will dictate to you, my employer told me as I dug with my hands against the waste and detritus of the floor of my hole. The midden was compacted but loose enough, the harder parts I broke with the bucket. When he heard me use it, he shouted at me to ease the materials out of the midden, not break them, so he might inspect it all in the light above.

The lantern went out during each night. I slept alongside its meagre and diminishing warmth in the crack in the side of the midden hill. He took the spent lantern in the morning and refilled it for me to dig alongside. The filled lantern came down on the rope already lit. I will dictate, he said, and I listened waiting for the lantern. When you are returned, I will dictate. I saw myself on the surface taking his dictation, learning of the midden. I will dictate, my employer told me with each return of the light. When on the surface I will tell you about the midden and its layering. I have the buckets tipped in a line, a chronology, their contents classified. I will tell you what they tell, my employer told me. When you return, I will tell you the contents of the midden.

I thought only of what he told me, of what he said would happen after, as I dug, as I waited for the lantern, as I woke when the crack was black and so not a crack only a memory of it being there. I thought of being on the surface, receiving his dictation, as I fell asleep again against the side and as I paused when the crack was lit. I thought of the telling of the midden with the sky above me, no crack, a sky across its full span, lighting the land around me where I would sit, taking his dictation down, writing our report. I thought of sitting on the surface, the midden below us long left, the excavation complete and no return to it. The thought of writing in the light was all I could imagine against this digging in the dark.

The midden, as I would come to write, documents everything every culture has expelled from itself. The shells you returned to me were mixed with all manner of fragments, my employer said. These were not merely broken and discarded objects that were dropped there because they had outlived their usefulness, he dictated. The shells themselves were not thrown in because this was a convenient place to drop them down. What culture hauls its waste to a fissure like this, at such a height, he asked—and had me write—simply for the purposes of disposal. This is not a convenient place to visit. This fissure in the earth drew them to it, my employer dictated. There is no other explaining the enormous breadth of cultural detritus it contains. Those living nearby knew the fissure well by the traffic of peoples it attracted across the sea, and before that, by the peoples it drew in from across the plains. I know, he admitted—and I wrote—it is improbable, he said. I know it makes no sense to think they travelled from such distances and over such extended periods of time. The migration of the peoples of the earth to this void in the crust over so many thousands of years must have left its trace. It should be possible to see some account of this extended and repeated trip that gathered all peoples or at least their representatives in annual, biannual, perennial cycles to tip in their waste. These considerable, prolonged migrations should be visible in recorded history. But nowhere is it written, and so it cannot be true. But you yourself have seen the midden hill, he said to me, you have excavated its contents, you have lived there within its strata, and so surely you must know as I do that there is no other accounting for its presence. Perhaps you do not know precisely what you dug, my employer had me write. Perhaps you did not see in the feeble light of your lantern what your hands eased out from the dirt you dug at, my employer went on. Did you not notice the bone in the shells you scraped out, he said, the remains of defiled, sacrificial animals thrown in the fissure, discarded uneaten, their bones uncut. These were not just pigs and rock badgers and pigmy goats or the unplucked bodies of frigates and night hawks, nor were they merely the remains of self-defiling hoopoes still arranged around the carcases of their young, or things that go on their bellies and things that do not, or things that swarm and solitaries that cannot, or creatures that lick between their legs and those that have no tongues at all to lick with, but defiled humans too, including those who carried the carcases of their abominations to the pit and fell in behind them. You returned fragments of daughters and fragments of sons from your excavation, he said. You returned pieces of jugs that were used to clean the dead, urns that contained viscera and growths cut out of the head, as well as bowls that held the puss that was drained from the suppurating wounds of the faithful and the blood of human sacrifices drunk and then spat into the cut. The midden contains all defilements, all forbidden objects, all expulsions. It holds all previous orderings of the cosmos that all cultures have seen to organise by determining what is clean and unclean, pure and impure, safe or dangerous, admissible or loathsome. The dirt and waste expelled here functioned to arrange experience and make it predictable. It served to combat the inherent untidiness of the universe they perceived and were confronted by. All humans have dropped their dirt here, their waste, those things they considered needless, or irksome, or worrisome, or troubling, my employer had me write and then looked at me for a little longer than usual. They have everywhere dropped their waste in this rift. The shedding of dirt is the functional and sacred, the profane and holy and ritualistic shedding of uncertainty and chaos. Everything every culture has ever decided to drive from before itself has found its way down. Their waste disappeared, he said, but did not vanish from their perception. Cultures have trod the earth to this point, have risen on the basis of this fissure in the crust, he said. They constructed their borders, the remit of their civilizational orders, by way of it, by establishing and re-establishing a sacred site for the absorption of waste. The body expels what it cannot absorb, is taught to be repelled by what it has done. It returns to that waste and turns it over, then tosses it out and flees from its stench, its abject textures. This body must be seen to exist in a condition of flight from what it has done. But like the city that exists only because of its management of dirt, the body of men only endures, can only thrive, by turning back and inspecting the ordure it creates. Cleanliness is the term that now obscures the sacredness of filth, my employer dictated. But cleanliness is only the latest ritualistic practice, the last rite we know before the rift. Advocates of cleanliness place order in relation to disorder, form in relation to deformation, and carry their expulsions to the crevice and throw tissues to the midden just as primitives climbed these slopes and threw their defilements into the void.

LAST WORDS.

My patient did not tell me how he escaped the midden and how he came to receive his dictation from the one he called his employer but led me to suspect it was by sliding down. The outer edges, he said, were banked up against the walls of the cavern from which passages led and with it the detritus of the midden scree travelled to a network of tunnels, empty lava flows and magma chambers, as well as further fissures in the rock caused by quakes. These narrow clefts were the natural well shafts down which the islanders lowered their buckets to gather the groundwater that seeped down and filled some of the magma chambers and empty flows forming pools, covered reservoirs, and lakes. Holding the lantern one might see how the midden waste was carried even here, although only the grey dust of it came furthest. The midden dust entered the water and billowed out, clouding its entrance points with each fresh influx carried by the groundwater flow. This is how the islanders came to drink the midden. The midden water, he told me, was their only reliable source of freshwater. Just as they drank the midden, so my patient went on to drink the midden, his employer drank the midden, the overseer and his servants too, all of them drinking from the midden water, there was nothing but midden water to drink. Anyone who lived on the island must drink the midden water and the midden dust, the dirt of centuries of rites, sacred filth, castings off, and efforts to command the chaos of the universe. We drank it all, he said. We drank their civilizational disorders, their heretic cosmogonies, their cast-offs, their notions of chaos. We drank their expulsions as each culture, clan, or family group built their world by way of their ejecta. Each well sampled a different era. The overseer drank from his single well when the brook was used up and very probably drank from the same well before it too. This river he once drank from was the only river on the surface of the island. It was the river he commanded and ruled over and dried by drinking it. Now he drank only from his own exclusive hole and the particular midden dust it communicated. The islanders supped differently, taking the layer of the midden that the water source they happened to be drinking drew its grey-travelled dust from. They roved between the wells of the island, passing across the minor fissures down which they lowered their buckets, taking the waters of one well, drinking one midden water and then the other, taking the expulsion of chaos from one era followed by the dust of expulsion from another, separated by centuries and civilizations, falls and rebirths of myth, abandonments and re-concoctions, un-countable deaths and births and rebirths and adjustments, forgettings and false recollections.

This he all said and told me as he lay. He told me about the midden dust and the magma chambers and the drinking of the grey dust of the midden hill and the consumption of expelled chaos as he called it or as he had his employer call it. His journey from the base of it, I gathered, so I thought, entailed leaving the midden hill and the midden chamber, the vast hollow in the centre of the island, by a small passage at its edge, at the foot, a series of channels and caverns after that, pools of water, dead lakes across which he waded or swam, and then a fissure upwards and a long ascent unaided by ropes. He returned to his employer, so he told me, and sat down for his dictation, his telling of what the midden told, and of what the islanders drank and he drank too. He sat for the words and the writing his employer had promised and he had imagined and fixated on as his memory of the surface and surface life. This memory and that promise sustained him below ground and compelled him upwards. That was all before his employer laid out the report for the islanders to see. His desire to receive dictation, his exit from the midden, was prior to when he fled from them, and fled from his employer, so he said.

My patient was weak again from the telling of the midden and from hearing my repetitions of what he told, words that prompted his words and caused him to speak. I made him speak yet again once more as I first caused him to progress from the sound of his choking, the birth of his language, to words that approximated my own. Since I had given him the definite article, the midden hill took form and acquired characteristics, materials that piled up upon it and grew the midden from the void of the island to its wellsprings. I repeated his words and rearranged them for him to repeat. He laid out his fist, the fist I bandaged, unbandaged, and watched as it remained closed. I repeated his words, he rearranged them for me to hear, his fist laid out, then turned the inner palm of it upwards. I looked at his gesture which preceded the end of his speech. I repeated his words, his mouth was shut, his fist was opened, its final opening to reveal its dirt. The midden, he said to me as I looked down at the grey congealment, skin-formed mouldings in the creases of his fist. The midden, he repeated. The midden, I said back, repeating his words as his eyes lowered and he raised his fist to the glass I held, my glass, and poured it in. I took these to be his last words and left him for the inn.

I was disoriented in walking to where the inn once stood. It was entirely gone down the cliff. The landlady was standing by the half hole it left, surrounded by much of the hamlet. As she stood there, I heard them recalling another house taken down some years before. The destruction of that house was preceded by ominous sounds, they said. Had she heard them too, they asked.

Was the collapse of the inn preceded by ominous sounds, for in several other cases these ominous sounds indicated an imminent collapse, and when some years before those inside heard these ominous sounds, they hurried in their nightclothes to the home of a neighbour. The sea-facing window fell out first, together with some stonework, and then so too the foundations. By morning the house overhung somewhat before its eventual fall to pieces. Did the inn come away like that, they asked, and was this how she survived. Or was it more like the house a few months back, the one which sat atop the ominous hole which appeared in the cliff and prompted its occupants to leave. Or was it more like the entire strip of houses which fell all apiece when the landlady was a girl, but without warning, some twenty houses or more sliding into the sea, and if so how did she survive it, they said, as the landlady stood and regarded the hole. If the inn fell all at once and without warning, as parts of the hamlet sometimes did, how did she make it out. Their attempts to imagine how she had done that went on about her, each attempt drawing from a previous account of a dwelling lost, the cumulative effect of which suggested to my mind that the hamlet dwellers had good experience of such things, and that the hamlet was in a state of inexorable if only gradual retreat into the cliffs of the narrow valley it backed against. Dwelling by dwelling as the sea ate pieces of it out, the hamlet was making its unplanned migration inward. I stood alongside her as they continued to ask how it was she survived, and as I heard them go on was reminded of the old man who told his grandson to always aim a little lower and produce a little less.

As the pressure mounted about us, I lent over and told the landlady of it, and how the grandfather shouted up through the hatch to the attic, It is better not to encourage the imagination, overly, and Silence is better than words, but if words must be used, they should always aim for a little less of themselves. These were the words the old man used, or something of the sort. I suspect the old man continued this advice as he took my own and began to weaken the ceiling above the bedchamber, readying that ceiling for its collapse. As the man above continued to believe in those places his fancy might take him, and so continued to place his hope in words, the man below readied the stage that would bring his fancy to a halt.

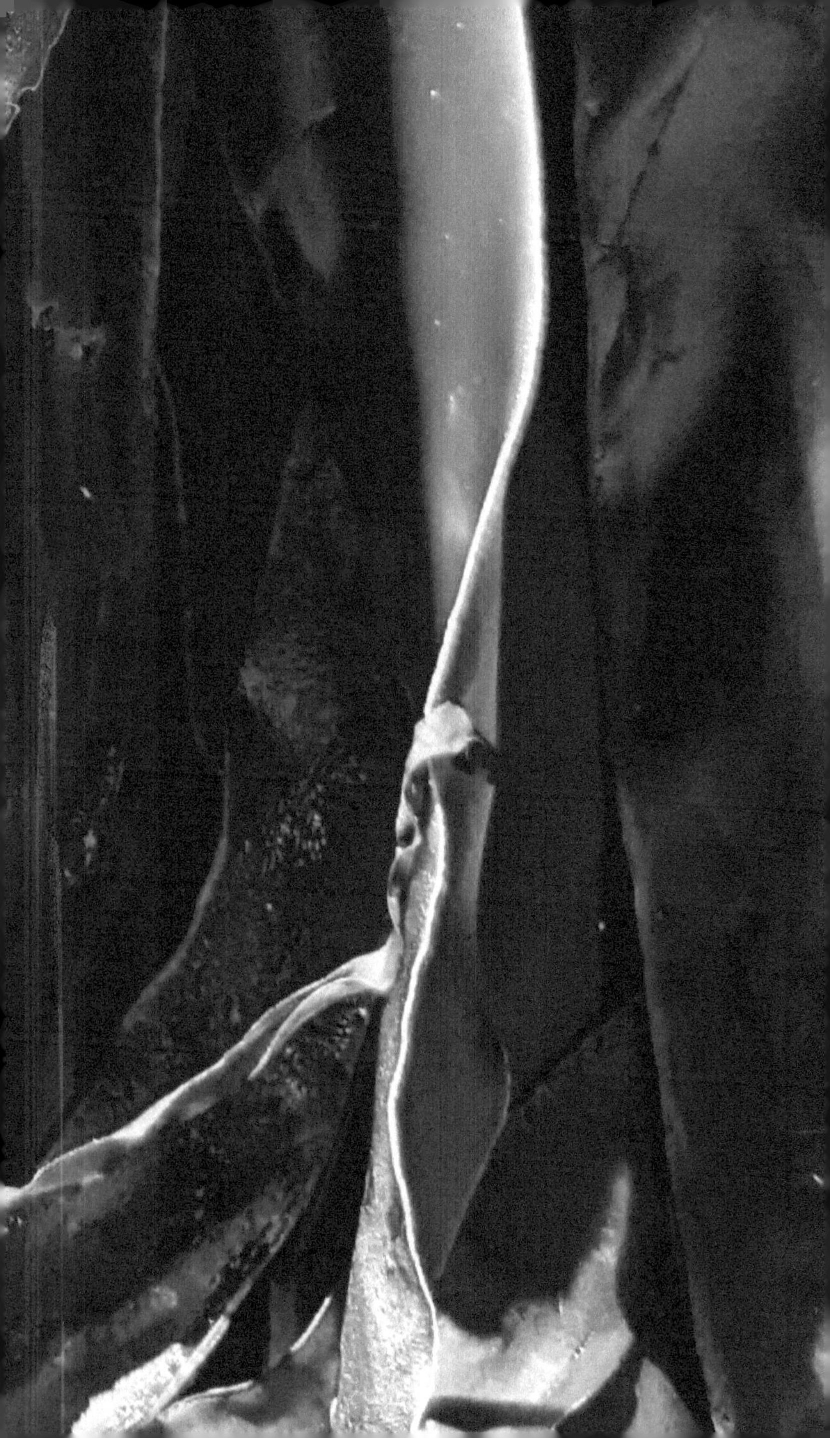

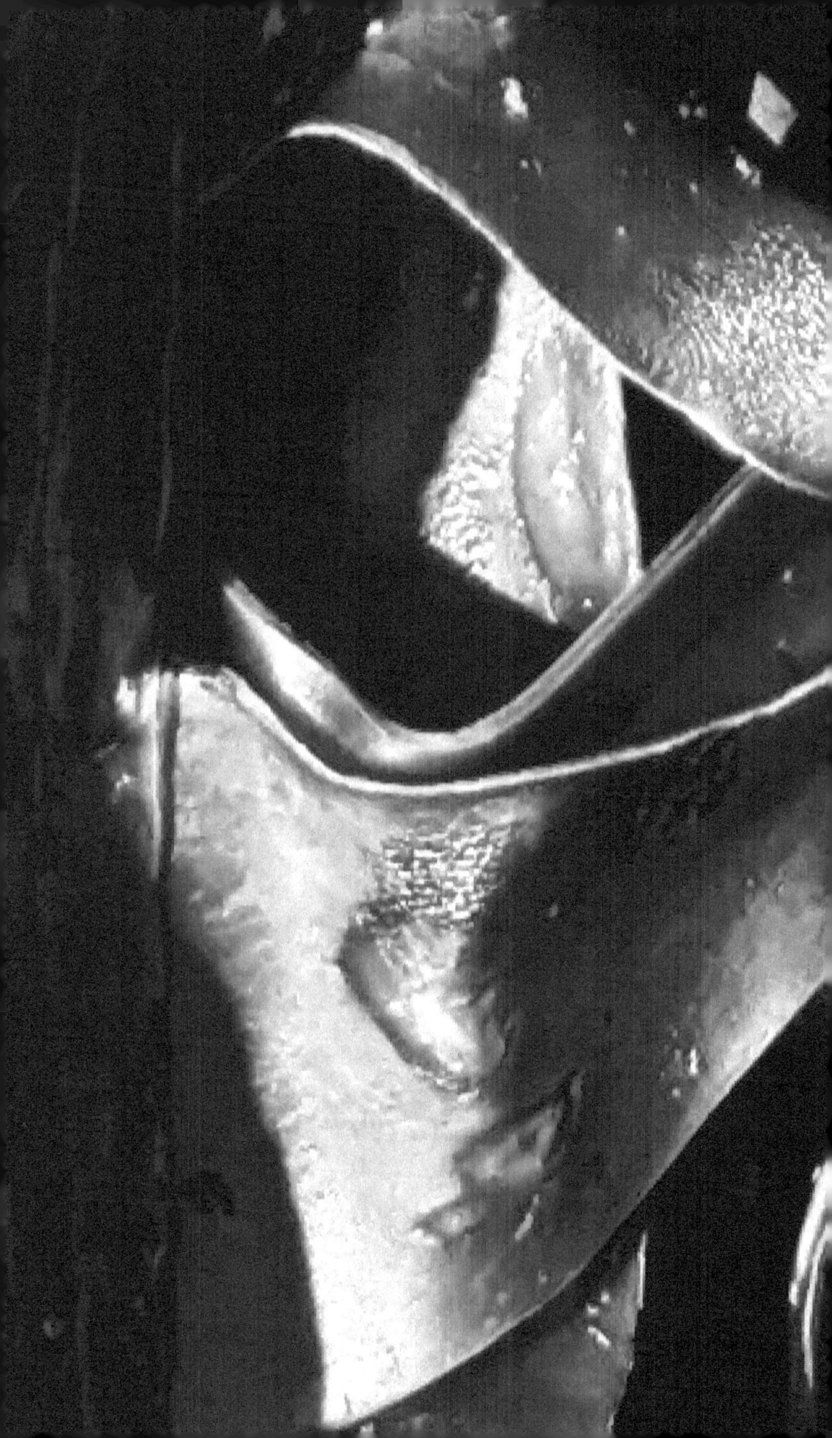

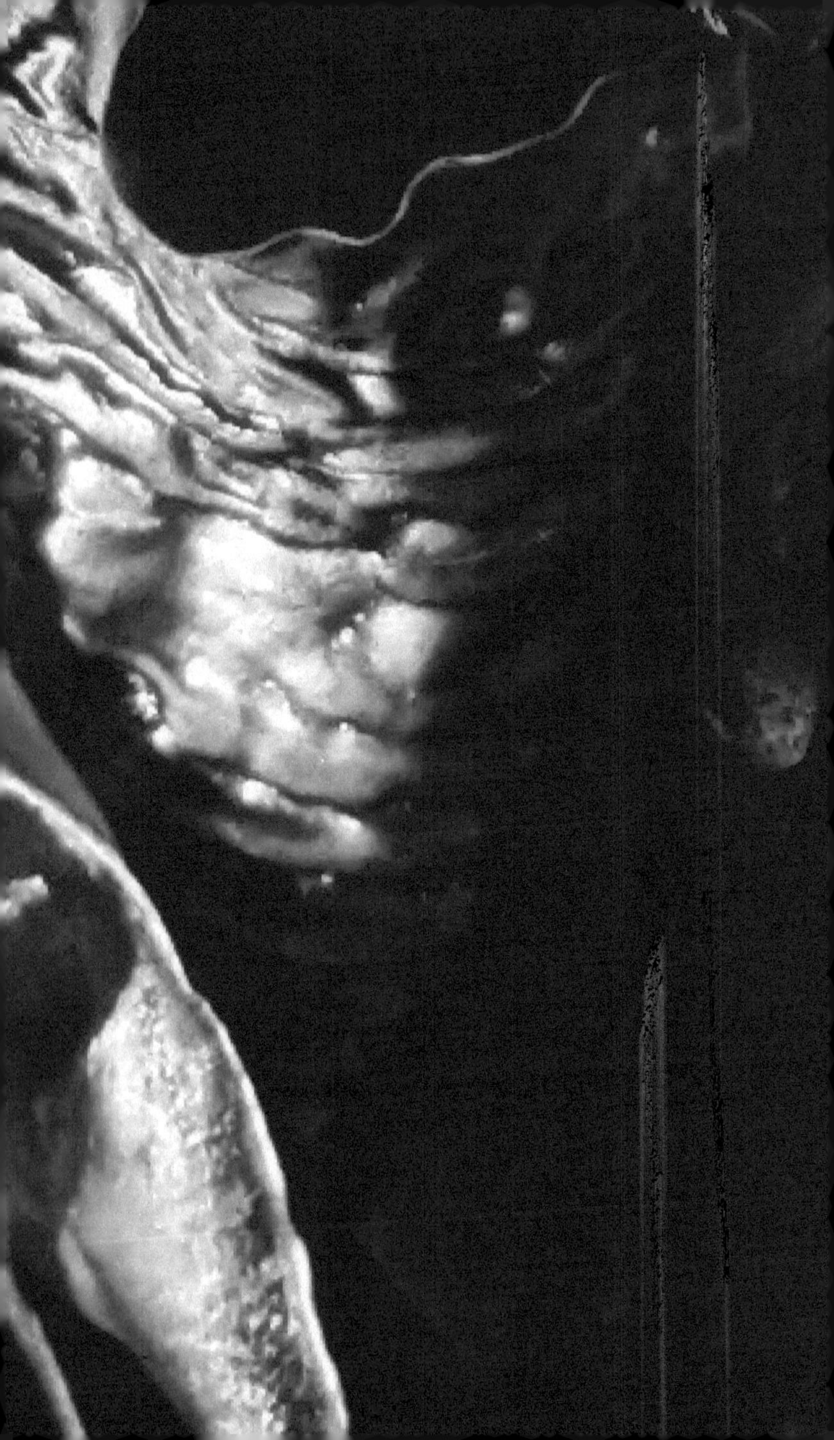

SCHISM²